ABOUT THIS BOOK

The highly anticipated sequel to *Saving Infiniti*—can Joe find Infiniti again or is she lost to him forever?

Joe Greg has reunited with his soul mate Infiniti Clausman only to lose her in a cruel twist of fate. Separated by time and space—and a memory ward that has wiped him from her mind—he vows to do whatever he can to find her, but so far nothing has worked. Believing he'll never be able to see her again, he starts losing all sense of himself. Worse than that, he can't shake the growing feeling that Infiniti's life is in danger . . . again.

Infiniti Clausman is trying to make the most of summer, but something isn't quite right. She feels like she's stuck, as if she can't move on, as if she's missing something or someone. She dismisses the sensation, calling it a case of the graduation blues, but when her psychic neighbor tells her about a quantum event that's been happening since the Cold Moon last December, Infiniti can't ignore the feelings any longer.

Soul mates separated. Memories forgotten. Time slipping. Joe must find Infiniti before it's too late—or he might lose her again, this time for good.

HAVENWOOD FALLS HIGH BOOKS

Written in the Stars by Kallie Ross

Reawakened by Morgan Wylie

The Fall by Kristen Yard

Somewhere Within by Amy Hale

Awaken the Soul by Michele G. Miller

Bound by Shadows by Cameo Renae

Fata Morgana by E.J. Fechenda

Forever Emeline by Katie M. John

Reclamation by AnnaLisa Grant

Avenoir by Daniele Lanzarotta

Avenge the Heart by Michele G. Miller

Curse the Night by R.K. Ryals

Blood & Iron by Amy Hale

Shadows & Spells by Cameo Renae

Falling Deep by J.L. Weil

Saving Infiniti by Rose Garcia

Willful by Liz Ferry

Cast in Moonlight by Ali Winters

Promise the Moon by Kallie Ross

Blurred Lines by Daniele Lanzarotta

Ascending Darkness by J.L. Weil

Finding Infiniti by Rose Garcia

Unicorn's Lament by Megan Linski

Paper Bird by Amy Richie

Predestined by Valia Lind

Rediscovered by Morgan Wylie

Ashes of Fate by Apryl Baker

Stay up to date at www.HavenwoodFalls.com

ALSO BY ROSE GARCIA

FINAL LIFE

FINDING INFINITI

A HAVENWOOD FALLS HIGH NOVELLA

ROSE GARCIA

To everyone who believes in second chances.

CHAPTER 1

*J*oe Greg studied every detail of Infiniti Clausman, desperate to sear her image in his brain because he didn't know if he'd be able to find her once she left Havenwood Falls. Long dark hair, ivory skin, the most gorgeous face he'd ever seen. She had time traveled with a Transhuman guy named Fleet from Houston to Havenwood Falls so she could find a protection spell. With their mission complete, they were about to return to their proper place and time, and Joe could hardly bear it. Her magnetic beauty had sparked a connection deep within him, so deep that he was called to her and would be bound to her forever—a wolf shifter and a human. Together against all odds, yet about to be separated in a cruel twist of fate. He knew he'd never be the same without her.

Her lips parted, as if she wanted to say something, just before she vanished from view.

"Infiniti!"

Joe dashed to the spot where she had been standing. Dust particles from Fleet's supernatural energy stream floated in the air. A warm electrical charge filled the cool space. Joe glanced around, as if they'd reappear, but they didn't.

They were gone. She was gone.

Heartbreaking silence filled the room.

"I'm very sorry, Joe," Ms. Howe said in a low voice, still clutching the book she had used to cast her protection spell on Infiniti.

Joe nodded, his heart crumbling. A lump the size of a football lodged in his throat. He felt as if a piece of him had been ripped away. And he didn't know if he'd ever get it back.

"I'll let you have a minute," Ms. Howe added, leaving the room.

Joe couldn't remember the last time he had cried, but watching Infiniti disappear brought hot tears to his eyes. He rubbed them away with the back of his hands, forcing himself not to lose it.

Not here anyway.

He tucked his crutch under his arm, his body throbbing with pain from the wild wolf attack at the Mills Mansion during the Cold Moon Ball earlier. He drew in a deep breath, then hobbled out of Ms. Howe's office and to the front of the herbal shop. He needed to get out of there. He kept his gaze down, avoiding eye contact.

"Thanks for everything, Ms. Howe."

"Sure thing, Joe."

He fumbled with the keys in his pocket as he painstakingly made it out of the shop and into his car. He sat there for a minute, letting the frigid air wrap around his body as the smell of the shop's herbs left his lungs, replaced by the scent of his newly washed car.

Twinkling white, red, and green holiday lights were strung up and down the street. Yet their cheerful and festive message fell flat on Joe. Despair had taken him over. Hours earlier, Infiniti was sitting next to him, dressed like a princess for the ball, and now she was gone. He leaned his head back against the headrest, thinking of their amazing kiss and the promise he had made to find her.

Could he really do it?

He started his car and headed home. Driving through the quiet streets of the town, a slew of memories exploded in his brain. A few months after Infiniti had vanished back in December 2012, he had a series of dreams of horrible things happening to her, incidents that all resulted in her death. Another car accident, being swept away by a tornado, drowning in the ocean, even catching on fire. He shuddered as dread worked its way through him.

He thought of that damn reaper, Shade StormIron, and his words: "The doll's soul still wants me. I can feel it. I'll be back in due time."

A blast of icy fear invaded his senses. Had they sent Infiniti back to 2012 only to die?

He slammed on his brakes and screeched to a halt. He made a U-turn in the middle of the road and sped back to the herbal shop. He parked the car, hopped out, and rushed over to Ms. Howe as she emerged from the door.

"It didn't work!"

She huddled into her long dark coat and wrapped her arms around herself. "What do you mean, it didn't work?"

"We sent Infiniti back to 2012, and she's going to die there! I know it!"

Ms. Howe looked away for a second, as if contemplating the possibility.

"Listen, Joe. I don't know if you're right or if you're wrong, but I do know a thing or two about destiny, and I can tell you that destiny cannot be changed. Not ever." She stared up at the night sky. "It's like telling the moon not to be bright. It simply can't be done." She flashed him a look of concerned sympathy. "So whatever will be, will be."

He looked down at the sidewalk, wracking his brain for a response, when an idea came to him.

"Okay, fine, I get that about destiny, I really do. But what if her coming here was another type of destiny? A way for the right destiny to counter the wrong destiny?" He stopped, thinking his words weren't making any sense, but went on anyway. "I mean, we didn't bring her here, yet she showed up needing our help. Maybe she needs our help again."

He hobbled forward, waiting for the red-haired witch to give him some sign of hope that she understood what he was saying and would help him.

She nodded but held a pensive look on her face. "Maybe she does, Joe. Maybe she does. But let's get through the holidays first, okay? We can take up this conversation later."

"Okay," Joe said, trying to calm his excitement. "That sounds great. I'll come by after the new year. Thank you, Ms. Howe."

Joe felt better, but there was no way he could wait until after the holiday break to do something about finding Infiniti. He got back in his car and drove home, his mind searching for his next move. Once home and in his room, he texted Kase, knowing he'd still be up.

Me: Dude

Kase: Sup

Me: Need your help

Kase: About the girl? Did it work? My dad told me

Joe wasn't surprised that Sheriff Ric had said something to Kase about what had happened to Infiniti, and he didn't mind. Kase was his best friend. He would've told him everything anyway.

Me: Yeah, I think. And now she's gone

Kase: Sorry

Me: It's ok. But I have an idea. Come over tmr. I'll fill you in

Kase: Ok

Joe set his phone down and lay on his bed, exhausted and feeling like crap. But more than anything, he was determined to find Infiniti Clausman. And no one could stop him.

He turned off his bedside lamp and eyed the streaks of moonlight that poured through the blinds of his window. His

4

mind swirled with different ideas of how he could find her when a soft knock sounded on his door.

"Joe, it's Mom. Can I come in?"

"Yeah, sure."

He sat up and switched his lamp back on. The soft light illuminated his blue-and-gray-hued room. His mom sat on the edge of his bed. Her long blond hair was wet from a recent shower.

"I heard you come in and wanted to check on you." She patted his leg and gave him a reassuring smile. "You okay?"

His fight with the wild wolf pack back at the Mills Mansion had left his body cut and bruised, but nothing could compare to the pain crushing his heart. He rubbed his head, masking his emotions, and focused instead on his physical pain.

"I'm fine. Just a little sore."

She gave him the all-knowing mom look. "I wasn't talking about your wounds, son."

"Oh," he murmured, not wanting to go there with his mom. "You mean Infiniti?"

"Yes, I mean Infiniti."

He thought of telling her his fears about Infiniti returning home only to die, but decided against it. She'd never let him try to find her. Neither would his dad. And really, he couldn't blame them. Try to find a time-traveling human girl he was called to? It was a crazy idea. Besides, they didn't even know he'd been called to her.

Joe shrugged. "She came here to do what she needed to do, and she's gone now."

His mom gave a slight nod. She patted his leg one more time and stood up to leave. "I'm very sorry, Joseph."

"Me too."

Alone again, Joe eased himself back into bed. He stared at the ceiling until the night crawled by and transformed to day. And when Kase finally showed up at his house later that morning, he hadn't slept a wink. He also hadn't formulated a plan for how he was going to find Infiniti.

"Dude," Kase said, looking his friend over. "You look like hell."

"You don't even know the half of it."

Joe limped his way down the hall, leading Kase to his room. He locked the door so they wouldn't be disturbed by his little brother, Boris.

Kase kept staring at Joe's bruised face. "My dad told me you were in a fight, but he didn't mention you got your butt kicked."

"I was swarmed. If that Transhuman guy Fleet hadn't shown up when he did, I don't know what would've happened."

Kase shook his head. "I wish I could've been there for you on that back patio instead of inside the Mills Mansion with Elle. I guess I was so wrapped up with her, I didn't even catch on that you needed help."

"Well, you can still help. That's why I texted you to come over."

Kase sat on the chair at Joe's desk. His leg bounced. He rubbed his hands together, ready for action. "Sure. Whatever you need."

Joe waited a few seconds before he continued.

"I need you to help me get to 2012."

Kase's eyes widened. He eyed Joe for a minute before laughing. "Uh, what?"

"Infiniti is in trouble. I felt it back in 2012 when she disappeared from the medical clinic, and I feel it again now. So I need to go to her. Right away. Before it's too late and something happens to her."

Joe kept a steady gaze on Kase, letting him know he wasn't kidding. The message finally sank in.

"You're serious?"

"Yeah, I am."

Joe moved across the room. He peered out the window and eyed the wintry landscape, wondering if Infiniti was still alive, when an idea came to him.

"I'm so stupid!" he called out. He snatched his laptop from his backpack and opened it on his bed. He ran a search for Infiniti Clausman Houston.

"Good idea!" Kase said, looking over his shoulder. "We can find her and help her from here. Time travel not required."

Joe's search turned up zero results. "Crap," he mumbled. "Nothing."

"Gimme that." Kase turned the laptop toward him. He typed Infiniti Clausman Texas. He clicked the search button. Still no results.

"Boys!" Joe's mom called from the other side of the door. "I've got some snacks if you're interested."

Joe's fingers hovered over the keys as his mind raced. There had to be a way to find Infiniti online. There just had to be. Or maybe there was no information on her because he was too late and she was dead.

His gut clenched tight. A knot formed in his throat.

"Be right there, Mrs. Greg!" Kase answered. He rested his hand on the laptop screen before closing it shut. He eyed his friend. "Joe, dude. She's back where she belongs, six years in the past. You need to let her go."

Joe knew right then and there that he couldn't involve Kase any further in his search. It'd be too dangerous, too risky. Plus, Kase didn't understand what it was like to be called to someone and have them ripped away. He'd have to go it alone. He forced a smile and put his hand on Kase's shoulder.

"You're right," he blew out, faking defeat. "I need to let her go."

"Exactly," Kase said with an encouraging smile. "Now, let's go eat."

Kase and Joe's little brother Boris dove into a mound of fritule pastries as if they hadn't eaten in days. Joe's mom made the donut-like fried Croatian delicacies every holiday. It was her most prized recipe that had been handed down from generation to generation. Joe usually had no problem matching their enthusiasm for food, especially for fritule, but this time he could barely finish a few bites. His stomach had twisted into a permanent knot, and he couldn't get his mind off Infiniti. Plus, exhaustion was beginning to set in after a night of life-altering events and no sleep.

Joe's mom caught on right away. She started clearing the kitchen table.

"Maybe you should rest, Joe. Take a nap or something. You did have quite the eventful evening."

"Yeah," Joe said, his eyelids so heavy he struggled to keep them open. "I could use a nap."

Kase got up and stretched. "Yep, I could use a nap, too. Thank you, Mrs. Greg." He patted Joe on the back. "See you later, dude."

Joe rubbed his throbbing shoulder, wincing a little from the sting of Kase's pat. He wondered when his wolf-shifter healing abilities would kick in as he retreated to his room. He eased himself onto his bed, his bones so sore he could hardly move. But as tired as he was, his mind was too busy to sleep just yet. Instead, he started formulating his plan. Go to Ms. Howe after the holiday and see if she'd help him. If she couldn't or wouldn't, then he'd have to find someone else to help him time travel to Infiniti. Question was, who could do it? And would they? He wasn't sure, but he was determined to find someone.

With a long yawn, he draped a blanket over himself. His body melded into the soft cotton while exhaustion took over and his brain finally shut off.

Early the next morning, Joe was back at it. He scoured the internet for any mention of a death of a Houston teen girl in 2012 but found nothing that matched Infiniti's description. He took that as a good sign and decided to go with the theory that she was still alive.

With his online search pretty much exhausted, he started looking into time travel. He spent days at the Sun and Moon

Academy library reading every book on magic and time travel he could find, but couldn't make any of the spells work for him. He thought of talking to Gallad Augustine or even Addie Beaumont to see if they'd help him, but their connections to the Court of the Sun and the Moon would be too risky. The last thing he needed was to cross the leaders of the town. His dad would be furious.

With the holiday break finally over, Joe went to see Ms. Howe at her herbal shop. She ended up giving him a long explanation for why he shouldn't meddle with fate and destiny. When school started, he subtly brought up the topic of time travel with some of his teachers, but nothing they mentioned helped him.

Days turned into weeks. Weeks morphed into months. Joe was beginning to think he'd never find Infiniti. Desperate and fresh out of ideas, he decided to change his tactic. Instead of searching for Infiniti in the past, he'd search for her in the present. He'd go up and down every single street in Houston if he had to. He didn't care if there was a six-year difference between them. Couples had age differences all the time. And in the larger scheme of things, six years was nothing. But what if he found her and she thought he was crazy? Or what if she was married? Or maybe she really was dead. He forced himself not to think of worst case scenarios. He had to keep trying until he found her.

But still, deep down, he couldn't shake the overriding feeling that he wouldn't be able to find her in the present because something horrible had happened to her in the past.

"Hang on, babe," he said as he started a fresh search on his laptop. "I'm coming."

This time he searched for flights to Houston for after graduation. He scribbled the prices on a piece of paper. Factoring in food and thinking he could sleep on park benches, he'd need at least eight hundred dollars. With the graduation money he thought he'd be getting, plus the money he'd be making over the summer, he'd have more than enough. As for his parents, he knew they'd be pissed, but he didn't care. He had to go.

The seasons changed from freezing to mild to sunny, and

before Joe knew it, the end of the school year had arrived. Graduation had come and gone. His friends were either making plans to go away for college or stay nearby and attend the new Sun and Moon Academy College of Supernatural Guardians. He had been invited to be a member of the inaugural class of the college, but had turned it down. He needed to focus on finding Infiniti. Nothing else mattered, and his flight to Houston couldn't come fast enough.

CHAPTER 2

*I*nfiniti blasted her music, eyeing the jam-packed closet her mother had been begging her for weeks to clean and organize. Kicking her shoes around, she started making a pile of stuff she didn't want anymore. She laughed at the absurdity of some of her older fashion choices.

"Well, look at that," she said, spying a worn-out shirt with a giant purple smiley face she had worn all the time when she was in middle school. "Cute and cringeworthy all at the same time."

She yanked the shirt from the hanger and tossed it in the give-away pile. The fabric bunched together into a pathetic looking bundle. Looking at the crumpled expression that now resembled a sad face instead of a smiley face, she couldn't help but feel sad, too. She scooped it up and held it close, feeling guilty at having dismissed it so harshly. Her mind replayed all the good memories from her youth—sleepovers, movie nights, roller skating parties. Now she had to go to college and get a job.

"Growing up sucks," she grumbled.

She folded the shirt neatly and placed it in her dresser with her other collectible tops. Fishing through the remainder of her wardrobe, she came across her senior year class shirt. It had a large rocket ship blasting into space on the front. On the back it said

Senior Odyssey 2013. The last time she had worn that shirt was the last day of school. She smiled, thinking of her fun times at Harmony High, then placed it with her smiley face shirt.

Senior year was over, summer had arrived, and college was around the corner. Infiniti wasn't ready at all. Something inside of her felt off. Weird. Like she was missing something. And it had all started around the Christmas break, right after her trip to Breckenridge, Colorado. Ever since that trip she'd been plagued with dreams of dying. She had searched for dream meanings and found an article that said dreaming of death signified transformation. The theory made perfect sense to her. She chalked up her nightmares to the whole college transition thing and dismissed her feelings as "graduation blues," yet the dread in the pit of her stomach seemed way more than that. She thought the strangeness would fade, but the sensation had only started to magnify.

"Stop being so emo," she ordered herself with a sigh, plopping down on her window seat.

She folded her legs, wrapped her arms around them, and gazed out at the sunny August day from her second-floor window. Branches and leaves from the tall oak outside crisscrossed her line of sight, providing the perfect view for her melancholy thoughts.

All of her friends had left for college already, and she had decided to go to the local community college at the last minute. She had told everyone, including her mom, that she had changed her mind because she wanted to get her basics out of the way, but deep down she felt as if she needed to stay in Houston for something. But what? Alone in her house, she was kind of regretting her decision.

Her stomach rumbled. "Food," she announced, perking up. "Yep, I need some food. Food makes everything better."

She started to get up when movement on the sidewalk caught her eye. It was a little girl she hadn't seen before. With her babysitting experience in the neighborhood, she thought she knew just about every kid in Rolling Lakes.

The girl was around five or so. She wore a white dress, and her long fair hair practically blended in with the material. The girl stopped, as if sensing Infiniti's stare. She shaded her eyes with one hand, looked up to where Infiniti was, then waved with her other hand.

Infiniti raised her hand in acknowledgment, watching as the girl dropped her hand and strolled up to her across-the-street-neighbor Jan's house. Her small frame slipped from view the closer she got to the door.

Infiniti searched her mind for any memory of Jan mentioning a granddaughter, but couldn't recall anything. She leaned down, so she could see better, but the overhang by Jan's front door obstructed her view.

"Huh," Infiniti muttered to herself, wondering who that was.

Her stomach issued a fresh reminder of its hunger. This time she obeyed the call. Traipsing down the stairs, she rounded the foyer when she glanced out her beveled-glass front door and saw the little girl again. She was standing by Jan's front door, facing Infiniti's house. She seemed to be looking straight at her.

Infiniti froze.

The little girl beckoned her to come over with a series of rapid hand gestures.

"Me?" Infiniti muttered out loud, although the little girl couldn't hear her. She moved closer to the door. She looked to the right and then to the left to see if anyone else was outside, but she didn't see anybody. When she brought her attention back to the girl, she was gone.

Infiniti gasped. A shiver raced down her spine. Was the girl a ghost? Even though she loved all things supernatural, deep down she was the biggest scaredy-cat she knew. She rested her hand on the brass doorknob. Should she go over there to investigate? And then she thought of Jan. Was there something wrong with her? She had known Jan her whole life. She had become like family to Infiniti and her mom over the years, especially since Infiniti's mom traveled a lot for work. If something was happening at Jan's, she had to help.

"Come on," she said out loud, mustering up her courage, telling herself that if it was a ghost, it was only a little girl. Plus, it was daylight. Nothing bad happened during the day, right?

She approached Jan's with caution. She rang the doorbell. She kept an eye on her surroundings when the door swung open.

"Infiniti, dear. How nice to see you," Jan said with a deep voice and a wide smile. Jan was a tall woman with deeply etched lines riddling her face and puffy gray hair that rested on her shoulders. Even though it was summer, she wore her usual long-sleeved shirt, long skirt, and socks with loafers.

"Hey, Jan." Infiniti scanned the crisp white walls and dark wood floors, wondering if the little girl she had seen would appear. "Is anyone . . . here with you?"

"No, it's just me. And Tinker, of course." Hearing her name, Jan's fluffy cat strolled into the room. "How about some tea? It's been a while since we've chatted, so I'd say we're due for a nice visit."

Tea and cookies was Jan's customary way of greeting visitors. Infiniti and her empty stomach had no complaints. "Sure. That'd be great."

"Is your mom away for business, dear?"

"Yeah. She'll be back tonight."

Infiniti followed Jan into the kitchen and took a seat at her small square-shaped wooden table. Jan chatted about the weather while she set a teapot on the stove and then disappeared into her walk-in pantry. She emerged with a plate of cookies and placed them in front of Infiniti.

"Well, my dear, it's been what, since the Cold Moon that we've had a proper visit?"

"That's right, the Cold Moon," Infiniti echoed, remembering how Jan had told her the full moon last December was called the Cold Moon. She also thought about the strangeness inside of her she'd been feeling ever since then. "It wasn't so long ago, yet it seems like a lifetime away."

"Interesting choice of words," Jan said.

Infiniti was about to take a bite of her cookie, but stopped. "What do you mean?"

The teapot whistled before Jan could respond. "Let me get that. Hold on to that thought, dear."

Jan removed the pot from the stove. She poured the boiling water into two dainty teacups. She put the cups on the table and offered Infiniti some tea bags. They started dunking their bags in the hot water, and soon the aroma of mint and herbs filled the air.

"Now, I didn't want to bother you, what with all your end-of-the-year school activities and graduation, but I've noticed a significant energy shift since the Cold Moon."

Infiniti's eyes grew wide. She leaned in. "You have?"

"Yes, I have." Jan sipped her tea. "You're pretty in tune with nature. Have you noticed anything odd?"

"Oh my god, yes!" Infiniti scooted her chair in closer, relieved that the bizarreness she'd been feeling wasn't just her. "I thought I was feeling all weird because I was graduating, but it wasn't making any sense. I spent my entire high school career looking forward to getting out of Houston, but now I feel like I can't leave. And I don't want to. Like I need to stay here for something, or even someone. It all started right after the holiday break, and it's only getting worse." She lowered her voice. "And by the way, I thought I saw a ghost girl or something outside your house just now." Infiniti let out a nervous laugh. "It's crazy, isn't it? I'm going crazy. Happy graduation, now you're nuts."

Jan put her thick wrinkly hand on Infiniti's small one and squeezed. "Nothing is crazy, especially not you."

Infiniti blew out a sigh of relief. "Okay, then what the heck is going on?"

Infiniti hoped Jan would have an answer. Jan was wise in a mystical way. She called herself a homegrown psychic and was into all things otherworldly. Together they'd used the Ouija board, dabbled in tarot cards, and even had fun with Jan's theory of everyone having nine soul lives on Earth. Jan had a way of explaining the unexplained, and Infiniti was ready for a rational explanation for everything.

Jan cleared her throat. "What color is Tinker's coat?"

Infiniti stitched her brows together, thinking for sure Jan would've asked about the girl she'd seen outside. But instead, she wanted to talk about the color of her cat?

"Huh?"

"Follow along with me on this, okay?" Jan paused for effect before repeating, "What color is my cat Tinker?"

Infiniti knew Tinker as well as if she'd been her own. She'd been playing with Tinker for years. She even took care of Tinker every time Jan went out of town. She loved that cat.

"Um, white, of course," Infiniti answered. "From her head to her toes. Pure white."

Jan lifted an eyebrow. She snapped her fingers a few times. "Tinker! Come, girl!"

Tinker trotted into the room. Infiniti scanned the feline—white body, a long fluffy white tail, and black paws. She did a double take. Black paws?

Infiniti's mouth dropped.

"W-w-w-hat?!" Infiniti stared at the cat, wondering if she was seeing things. "She's white . . . and black?"

"Yes," Jan acknowledged. "One day, I noticed she was different. Like something wasn't quite right with her. I couldn't put my finger on it, but then, as I studied her, I had a memory of her being all white."

Infiniti stared at Tinker and then back at Jan. She forced herself to follow Jan's explanation. "So . . . your memory didn't match reality?"

"Exactly, my dear." Jan's eyes took on a faraway look. "I've noticed differences with other things, too. I could've sworn the color of my favorite book was red, when in fact it is blue. Even the name of my favorite restaurant is spelled differently than I thought." She narrowed her attention on Infiniti. "It's subtle, small things someone might not recognize at first, but when added up with everything else, is actually quite significant."

Infiniti pushed the plate of snacks away, suddenly losing her appetite. "I-I-I don't know what to say. I mean, when I walked in, I saw Tinker, and I didn't notice anything out of the ordinary. But there she is," Infiniti gestured to Tinker, "with black paws."

"You didn't notice because your mind and your eyes were not in sync. And now that I've pointed it out to you, the truth has been unveiled."

"How is this even possible?" Infiniti continued staring at Tinker, as if she had come from another planet.

"I've been looking into it, and I believe there's been a quantum event." Jan paused for a long while before she went on. "I think we have slid into an alternate reality. A different timeline, if you will."

"Holy shit," Infiniti whispered. She bit her lip because she had never cussed in front of Jan. "Sorry."

"It's okay." Jan chuckled. "If there's any time to issue an expletive, this would be the time."

Infiniti sipped the tea, thinking it'd calm her, but it didn't. Her heart raced out of control while her mind started picking away at her life. She couldn't pinpoint any solid differences in anything else, other than Tink's differently colored paws staring her in the face, but the unease that had settled deep within her told her that Jan was right. The world was *off*.

"And the ghost girl," Jan said in a lowered voice. "I've seen her, too."

Infiniti sucked in a breath. She held it for a while before squeaking out, "You have?"

"I have indeed." Jan reached out for Infiniti's hand. She held it in a death grip. "Her name is Abigail, and she says you need to go back."

Infiniti's mind reeled. Her heart catapulted against her chest. She stared at her fingers that were turning purple from Jan's hold. "Go back where?"

Jan released her. "I don't know, my dear. She disappeared before she could explain." Jan looked up and away, as if lost in thought. "That was a few weeks ago. Despite my best efforts, I haven't seen her since."

The old-fashioned cuckoo clock in the kitchen started chiming.

"Oh my, the time!" Jan got up. She placed the teacups in the sink. "I'm so very sorry to cut our conversation short, but I have an appointment to get to. How about we chat again tomorrow?"

Infiniti rose to her feet while Jan bustled about. The earth was experiencing some weird timeline shift, a ghost girl named Abigail wanted her to go back to wherever, and now Jan had to leave for an appointment? Talk about terrible timing.

"I guess I'll come back tomorrow, then."

"Yes, tomorrow," Jan agreed. She ushered Infiniti to the front door. Stopping at the threshold, she put her hands on Infiniti's shoulders. "We'll figure this out. Easy peasy."

Infiniti gulped. Jan only said "easy peasy" when something was *not* easy peasy. As in the opposite of easy peasy. She wished Jan hadn't said that, because now she was freaked.

"Okay," Infiniti said. "See you then."

Once outside, Infiniti breathed in the warmth from the summer air, trying to erase the fear building inside of her.

"I'm cool," she said out loud. "Everything is totally cool. Easy peasy can sometimes actually mean easy peasy."

She looked down the street to the right and then to the left. Not seeing anyone, ghost or otherwise, she booked it back home, slammed the door behind her, and locked it.

She took out her phone and texted her mom.

Infiniti: What time ya coming home

She went to the kitchen and ripped open a bag of Flamin' Hot Cheetos. She shoved the fire-hot crispy goodness in her mouth and started crunching while keeping her eye on her phone.

Mom: Should be there around 9

Infiniti: K, see you then

Mom: Love you
Infiniti: Love you

She tucked her phone into her back pocket, then finished off her snack. She thought her favorite junk food would make her feel better, but it didn't. Fear of ghosts and quantum events swirled in her head.

"Okay, I'm not doing this," she commanded herself, pushing every eerie thought out of her brain. "Back to the closet."

She went up to her room, closed her door and her blinds, lit some incense, and started sorting through her clothes, telling herself everything was going to be okay.

Easy peasy.

CHAPTER 3

Fleet bolted upright in bed, panting from the nightmare he'd been having. He kicked off his covers, swung his legs over the edge of his bed, and planted his feet on the ground. He ran his fingers through his thick dark hair while his breathing settled. Eyeing his clock, he saw it was five in the morning.

"Son of a bitch."

Fleet knew there was no way he could go back to sleep, so he got up. He slipped on a white T-shirt and dark sweatpants and headed for the kitchen.

"Another dream?" Fleet's brother, Farrell, was standing by the coffee machine as it spewed hot brown liquid.

"Yeah, you too?"

"Yeah."

They were practically mirror images of each other, except Fleet had dark hair while Farrell had blond. They crossed their arms at almost the exact same time and waited for their brew to finish. When the machine sputtered out its last drops, they poured themselves two oversized mugs of coffee and sat on the sofa in the living room. Windows lined the back wall of their log cabin in the Michigan woods—the cabin they had called home for lifetimes.

"What did you dream about this time?" Farrell asked.

Fleet blew out a long breath. "Infiniti. She keeps popping up in my head. Always dying, always pleading for me to help her. Like a damn movie stuck on repeat." He peered out the windows, searching for any sign of daylight, but didn't see any. "What about you?"

Farrell kept his eyes down. "For me it's Dominique. Over and over."

Farrell never elaborated about his dreams of Dominique, and Fleet never asked. Too much had happened between the three of them, and he didn't need to know his brother's hidden thoughts.

Fleet rubbed his stubbled face, reminding himself that he and Farrell had agreed to stay away from Dominique, Trent, and Infiniti. But something about Tiny's pleas wouldn't let him go.

"What if I need to help her?" Fleet asked. "What if her story isn't finished?"

Farrell shifted and faced his brother. "What do you mean?"

"I don't know, and I can't explain it. But something inside me is telling me this is different. That she really does need my help."

Farrell let the idea sit with him for a few seconds. "But we agreed to stay away from them. Remember?"

"Yeah, yeah. I remember."

Fleet got up and faced the windows. After everything they'd been through with Dominique's final life, he didn't know why Infiniti of all people would somehow need his help. Infiniti had played a major role in Dominique's story, but everything was over now. And as far as he knew, she was safe and sound in Houston, probably getting ready for college.

"You helped Infiniti in Havenwood Falls."

Fleet spun around and saw Abigail. He recognized the ghost girl right away. He hadn't seen her in a while and had no idea what she was talking about.

"I helped Infiniti in Havenwood Falls?"

Transhumans knew about the supernatural town of Havenwood Falls without having any specific knowledge about it, other than it was located somewhere in Colorado. It was an agreement made between Transhumans and the founding members of the town in case the town ever needed their help. But Fleet had never stepped foot in the place. In fact, he didn't know of any Transhuman who had. Surely the girl was mistaken.

He threw Farrell a curious look. He could tell by the puzzled expression on his brother's face he didn't know what Abigail was talking about either.

"You must be confusing me with somebody else. I've never been to Havenwood Falls," Fleet said, approaching the girl with caution.

"Neither have I," Farrell added, on his feet now too and standing by Fleet's side.

Abigail pointed at Fleet. "You've been there, with Infiniti, though you don't remember it. She doesn't remember either. The town spelled you both to forget when you left," she said in her young ethereal voice. She looked away, as if dismissing that part of the conversation. "But that's not important right now. The important part is you need to go to her. To her house in Houston. She's in danger."

"She's in danger?" Fleet asked. "Explain."

Abigail's form started fading. "That's all I can say. The rest is up to you," she said as she shimmered out of view.

"Wait!" Fleet called out.

The small girl disappeared, leaving Fleet with a thousand questions and no answers. He eyed his brother. "That's just great. A cryptic message about a supernatural haven I've apparently been to but don't remember. And I have to help someone you and I agreed we'd stay away from."

Fleet studied his brother, waiting for him to say something.

"You need to go to her," Farrell said after a while. "Your dreams and now Abigail appearing and saying Infiniti needs you? It can't be a coincidence."

Fleet knew Farrell was right. There was no such thing as

coincidence. "What about Havenwood Falls? What do you make of that?"

Farrell shrugged his shoulders. "I guess you'll figure it out as you go along."

Fleet lowered his coffee mug. "Wait a minute. You're not coming with me?"

Farrell looked away, and Fleet knew why. It was Dominique, but Fleet knew his brother didn't want to say.

"I should stay here," Farrell explained. "If Infiniti needs you, then maybe," he paused, "someone else will need me."

Fleet placed his hand on Farrell's shoulder, letting his brother off the hook. "Understood. I'll go it alone. I'll call for you if I need backup."

Fleet stood with his brother in silence while streaks of morning sunlight began to filter into the woodsy cabin. Fleet studied the budding summer day as his mind cluttered with everything he'd been through—love, death, betrayal. So much pain and hurt over so many lifetimes. He thought it was all over, but now Tiny needed him. He couldn't even imagine what for, but he needed to see it through.

"Should I zap over there? Or drive?" he asked Farrell. They had decided to use their abilities only when necessary so they could keep off the grid. He wondered if the call to aid Tiny qualified as necessary.

"I think you should err on the side of caution and drive. Besides, you may need a car while you're there."

"You're right. I can make it there by nightfall if I drive straight through." He rubbed the back of his neck. "Guess I should go pack."

Back in his room, Fleet got dressed in a hurry, anxious to get on the road. He threw some stuff in a duffel bag, then did a last minute scan of his room to make sure he wasn't forgetting anything. Ready for the drive to Houston, he said a quick goodbye to his brother and left.

Fleet drove into the day, his mind picking apart his lifetimes.

He searched for any clue about why Tiny would need his help now and why Abigail said he'd been to Havenwood Falls when he had no recollection of it. None of it made any sense. He only hoped that whatever was going on wouldn't be that bad.

But he knew better.

Shit always happened to him.

CHAPTER 4

*G*azing out his bedroom window at the bright August sky, Joe couldn't believe so much time had passed since Infiniti left Havenwood Falls. He remembered the Cold Moon Ball as if it were yesterday. He closed his eyes, picturing blankets of snow covering the town, holiday decorations that sprinkled homes and businesses, Infiniti looking beautiful in her purple dress, and the amazing kiss they had shared.

He opened his eyes, returning to reality and the backpack on the floor he'd been packing for his trip to Houston in the morning. He'd spent the summer saving money and preparing, and the time to go was finally arriving. Maps of the massive Texas city were strewn about his bed. Most were of neighborhoods and streets; others were of major roads and highways. He had planned his search in grids, focusing on the innermost parts of the city first and then branching out. He hoped it wouldn't take too long to catch her scent, but he needed to be prepared for a long stay just in case.

He folded the maps carefully and stuffed them in the inside pocket of his backpack. He followed that with clothes and toiletries. With his pack loaded, he took the plane ticket he had purchased from a travel agent a few towns over and placed it in the oversized envelope that held enough cash to last him a few weeks.

A light rap sounded at his door. Joe froze. He eyed his things and started scooping everything up.

"Joe? It's Mom. Can I come in?"

"One sec," he said, shoving his pack in the back of his closet. He threw a blanket over it for good measure.

Trying to look as casual as possible, as if he hadn't just been planning his big getaway, he opened the door.

"Hey, Mom. What's up?"

She was wearing jeans and a floral printed blouse. Her long blond hair was pulled up in a ponytail. "I just got a call from Dr. Underwood. He wants you to come in today for a checkup. Says he cleared some room in his schedule for you."

"A checkup? What for?"

Even though he had asked, Joe knew the reason. He'd been wasting away for months. His clothes hung loose. He hadn't had a haircut or a shave since graduation, though he was meaning to clean up before his flight to Houston.

"Well," his mom said, fidgeting with her hands, "I saw Dr. Underwood earlier today at Coffee Haven. He asked me how you were doing. I told him you still had your limp from the scuffle at the Cold Moon Ball."

"Mom, why did you say anything? It's just a limp. It's no big deal."

"It should've gone away by now, son." She eyed him with determination. "You know I'm right."

Joe's hand went to his leg. Deep down he'd been worrying about why he hadn't fully healed, and it seemed his mom had the same concerns. Probably his dad, too. Guilt struck him at the pain he knew she and his dad would go through when he left. The least he could do was go with her to the doc. Besides, maybe the doc could help him. Having a limp was sure to slow down his search.

"Fine," he said. "I'll go. Do I have time to shower?"

"Sure. I'll be waiting in the kitchen. But please don't take too long, okay?"

"Yeah, okay."

Standing in the hot stream of water, Joe's mind rehearsed everything he needed to do to leave town. Fake needing to leave early for a hike, head to the bus station for a ride to Montrose, Colorado, then catch his flight from there. He'd text his parents and let them know what he'd done once he made it to Houston.

When he finished his shower, he dried off and stood in front of the mirror.

"Damn," he whispered, taking a good look at his reflection for the first time in a while. He hardly recognized himself. His usually short-cropped blond hair had grown so much it covered his ears and hung in his eyes. He leaned forward, rubbing the scruff on his face. It wasn't a full beard, but pretty close. Assuming Infiniti would have any chance of remembering him, it wouldn't be like this.

Lathering up his face with shaving cream, he started taking off the facial hair. And when he finished, he thought he looked more like himself. The next thing he needed was a haircut. Maybe he could get one after seeing the doc.

Dressed and ready, Joe got in the car with his mom. She tried to strike up a conversation with Joe about his friends and what they had been up to, but there wasn't much to say, since he hadn't really seen them in a while. Eventually, he and his mom resorted to silence as their small-talk faded.

After a few minutes, the Medical Center came into view. Only a few cars lined the parking lot of the converted white house with blue trim. Joe hoped that meant his appointment would be quick. Down the way, he spotted the shopping center and Burger Bar. He thought of how Infiniti had ended up at the clinic in December and then wandered down to Burger Bar because she was hungry and needed a phone. That was before she found out she had time traveled.

"You hungry?" Joe's mom must've followed his line of sight. Optimistic yet subtle enthusiasm laced her voice. "Want to get a burger when we're finished?"

Joe had no appetite, but didn't want to disappoint her. "Yeah, maybe." He ruffled his hair. "What I could really use, though, is a haircut."

His mom parked the car with a smile on her face. "A possible burger and a haircut. Sounds like a plan."

They were escorted to an exam room in the back of the clinic. Joe's mom took a seat on the chair in the corner of the room.

"Mom, really? I'm not a kid anymore. I got this."

"Oh." She got up, looking a little surprised. "Sure, of course. I'll be out in the lobby."

Joe paced about the room for only a few seconds when a knock sounded on the door and in walked Dr. Jasper Underwood. He had salt-and-pepper hair and wore khaki pants with a button-down shirt and a white lab coat. He held a chart in one hand and extended his other hand for a shake.

"Joseph," he said with a warm smile and strong grip. "Thank you for coming to see me today. And congratulations on graduating!"

"Thanks, Doc."

"What are your plans after summer?"

"I'll be taking online college classes and working full time with Sheriff Kasun."

"You won't be going to the new college? The Sun and Moon Academy College of…" The doc's voice trailed off. He tapped his forehead, searching for the full name of the new school.

"…Of Supernatural Guardians. No, I'm not. There's too much work to be done here," Joe explained, issuing the canned response he used any time someone asked him about his college plans.

"Ah, a young man of duty. I admire that, Joseph."

Dr. Underwood patted the paper-lined exam table, and Joseph hopped on. The doc rolled a stool over from the corner of the room and took a seat. He opened the chart and started reading to himself.

"I saw you back in December after that event with the wild wolf pack, then three months later to check on your healing. And then this morning, I ran into your mother at the coffee shop. She says you're still limping. Does that sum it up?"

"Yeah," Joe said. "Pretty much."

"Hmm," the doc said, rubbing his chin. "Let's do all the regular stuff before we look at that leg, shall we?"

Joe rubbed his hand on his jeans. "Okay."

The doc set his chart down. "I'm going to give it to you straight, Joseph. You're not looking so hot. Though I do appreciate the fresh shave." He winked. "Other than the limp, how are you feeling?"

Joe knew he wasn't looking his best, but hearing the doc say something out loud made him think he looked way worse than he thought.

"I'm feeling all right."

Dr. Underwood took the blood pressure cuff from the hook on the wall. He wrapped the arm band around Joe's bicep and started pumping.

"You've been struggling since your scuffle at the Cold Moon Ball. Is that right?"

"Um, yeah. That's right."

"And you don't seem to be getting better?"

Joe thought of hiding the truth, but then decided to be honest. "No. Not really."

Joe's arm was squeezed tight until the arm band started releasing in intervals. Dr. Underwood watched the numbers. He removed the cuff and hung it back on the wall where it belonged.

"Numbers are low, Joseph."

A twinge of panic struck Joe. "Is that bad?"

"Well, for your age not necessarily. You may just be a little dehydrated, but let's finish the exam." Dr. Underwood motioned toward the scale. "Let's get your weight."

Joe walked across the room. He stared at the scale for a few seconds before stepping onto it slowly. The numbers blinked until they stopped on a weight that was almost fifteen pounds below his normal.

Dr. Underwood made a notation in the file. "Are you trying to lose weight?"

"No. I'm just not as hungry as I used to be, I guess."

"I see," Dr. Underwood mumbled, scribbling on the chart. "Hop back up on the table."

Dr. Underwood held Joe's wrist and started taking his pulse. "Would you say your limp is the same, better, or worse since the Cold Moon Ball?"

"Ummm," Joe had been trying to hide his limp for months, but hadn't really thought of it in terms of comparing it to the initial injury. He shrugged. "I guess it's a little better?"

The doc released his hold. He scribbled more notes, then took a penlight from his medical coat pocket and shined it in Joe's eyes. When he finished, he dropped the light back where it belonged.

"Pulse is a little elevated, but your eyes are dilating fine."

Joe breathed a sigh of relief. "That's good at least."

Dr. Underwood set his stuff aside. He crossed his arms. His usual positive facade gave way to a serious look.

"Good is a relative term. If you were an ordinary young man, I'd say you were simply lovesick. But you're not an ordinary young man. You're a wolf shifter. Your wounds from that attack should've healed months ago, and they haven't."

Joe wondered if there was something *really* wrong with him. He'd heard of other shifters going insane when separated from their mates, but he'd never heard of it happening to anyone in his pack. Maybe something else happened to his pack, like some sort of slow and painful deterioration. He let out a nervous laugh, hoping he was wrong.

"Do I need to be worried?"

"The girl, the time traveler, you were called to her—am I correct?"

Joe's face grew hot. The image of Infiniti's bloodied body at the car wreck flashed before his eyes. Other than Fleet, he hadn't told anyone about his connection to Infiniti.

"Yeah, I was twelve when it happened."

Dr. Underwood rubbed his chin. "Lovesickness is a real thing, Joseph. It can cause all kinds of ailments, similar to the ones you're experiencing—weight loss, withdrawal, and even improper healing when the body is compromised."

"Wait a minute," Joe cut in. His mind raced, thinking of how he had felt when Infiniti disappeared in 2012. She had most definitely plagued his thoughts and dreams, but he had never gotten sick. "Why am I feeling all this now and not then?"

Dr. Underwood stitched his brows together. "Good question, Joseph. I surmise it's because you were so young the first time she was here. Plus, she disappeared quickly. But this go around you're much older, and you spent significant quality time with her. And I'm assuming she bonded with you in turn. Am I right?"

Joe thought of their kiss and how Infiniti had begged him to find her. "Yeah, you're right." His heart hurt, as in actual physical pain. The type of pain he knew would never go away. "So I'm lovesick."

"You are indeed. But the difficulty with someone like you being lovesick is that you are not a normal young man. You are a wolf shifter, and you've lost your mate. Some wolf shifters adjust to a loss like that and move on. Others . . ."

Dr. Underwood's voice trailed off as he appeared to be searching for the right word.

Joe sat forward. "Others what?" he prompted, needing to hear the truth.

"Others don't recover."

Joe gulped as ripples of goose bumps raced across his skin. He feared not being able to make it to Houston to look for Infiniti. And then he envisioned a tombstone with his name on it.

"Doc, what do you mean? Don't recover? As in—"

The door swung open, and Joe's dad entered the room. He

was almost an exact replica of Joe, tall with blond hair. His build was thick and muscular. Joe used to be pretty muscular, too. Now he felt like skin and bones. He was wearing his usual patrol jeans, tucked-in Henley shirt, and leather jacket. He even had his gun still strapped at his waist. Joe's mom came in right behind him. They both wore worried expressions, but Joe's dad quickly erased his. He patted Joe's shoulder, then shook Dr. Underwood's hand.

"Sorry I'm late. Had to finish up a report before I could leave the station."

"That's okay, Ivan. I was just about to ask Katarina to come back in. You both need to be in the exam room for this next part."

"Dad?" Joe looked from his mom to his dad. "I didn't know you were coming."

"We're all in this together, son."

All in this together? Joe's stomach tightened even more. He thought for sure he was dying, and they all knew it.

Dr. Underwood motioned for his parents to shut the door behind them. "I was about to explain to Joseph how some wolf shifters don't recover when they lose their mates."

"I knew it," Joe's mom uttered.

"Wait a minute," Joe said. "Knew what? That I was called to Infiniti or that I'm dying?"

"No, no, no," Dr. Underwood cut in with an apologetic tone. "Joseph, you are frail and weak and could possibly never regain your robust nature, but to say you're dying would be quite the worst case scenario."

"But a possible scenario nonetheless?" Joe asked.

"Joseph," the doc said, meeting him eye to eye. "Right now, you are not dying."

The doc's words fell far short of making him feel better, because saying *right now you are not dying* was not the same as saying *you are not dying*. But Joe figured he'd take what he could get. Glossing over his parents suspecting he was called to Infiniti, thinking that detail was not that important under the circumstances, he wondered what it meant to never regain his robust nature.

"Fine. I'm not dying right now, but I'm gonna be skinny with a limp and feel lost and hopeless the rest of my life? And maybe die somewhere down the road? I don't think so."

He didn't want to die, not at all. But he also didn't want to continue living like he had for the last few months. That's why he had to go to Houston.

"We are all in agreement that something needs to be done, Joseph," his mom said.

"Dr. Underwood is going to try to heal you," his dad tacked on with a hopeful tone.

Joe perked up. He studied the doc's navy-colored eyes. He hadn't even thought about the doc being a fae but now was thinking of nothing else.

"That's right. Doc, you can heal me!"

Excitement at being strong and healthy again exploded inside of him. Determination spread through his veins. If he got well, he'd have a better chance at finding Infiniti.

Joe clapped his hands together. "Let's do it."

"All right," Dr. Underwood said with a smile. "Let's give it a go. All you need to do is be still, okay?"

Joe nodded. "Be still. Got it."

Dr. Underwood raised his hands. He brought them to either side of Joe's head, right at the temples. He closed his eyes. The touch warmed Joe's skin ever so slightly.

"I'm reading your body," Dr. Underwood explained. "Like a scan."

"Okay," Joe whispered.

After a few long seconds in that position, the doc moved his hands down. He rested them on Joe's chest, right over his heart. Joe looked down and saw light glowing all around the doc's hands. A slight warmth penetrated through his shirt, as if someone had lit a fire before him. He watched as the glow waned, then flickered, then waned again, as if struggling to hold steady.

Joe didn't think that was supposed to be happening.

He brought his gaze back up to the doc and saw his face straining from effort. His lips quivered. The heat on Joe's skin magnified until it almost burned. Joe held his breath, wondering if he should break contact, when the doc dropped his hands with a grunt.

"Doc, are you okay?"

"Yes, I'm fine." Dr. Underwood took a handkerchief out of his pocket and wiped his brow. "But I'm sorry to say I was unsuccessful. I'm very sorry, Joseph. Seems your heartbreak is a lot deeper than I thought."

A heavy silence filled the room as Joe considered the implication of Dr. Underwood being unable to heal him. Did that mean the worst case scenario was an actual possibility now? Had his death sentence kicked in? He thought so, but didn't want to say it out loud. Saying it made it real.

Joe patted his chest, just to make sure he was okay. "Well, now what?"

"Plan B," Dr. Underwood announced.

Joe raised his brows. He eyed his parents, catching on that they and the doc had been plotting this whole visit for a while. A plan A and a plan B didn't just happen.

"What's plan B?'

The doc crossed his arms. "In the event the healing didn't work, your parents and I discussed petitioning the Court to help you find Infiniti."

Joe hopped off the table. He smiled with excitement and disbelief. If they could convince the Court of the Sun and the Moon to help him, the governing body of the town and the supernaturals, his search would be a whole lot easier.

"Really?"

"Yes, really." His dad smiled back. "Your mom and I couldn't bear to see you like this any longer."

"Well, let's go. Now. To the Court. Let's do this!"

Dr. Underwood shushed Joe. "I know you're excited, Joseph, but don't forget we have other patients in the clinic."

"Oh, that's right. Sorry." Joe shrugged but couldn't keep the smile off his face.

"And we just can't waltz into the Court with something like this," Joe's dad said in a lowered tone. "We need a Court hearing and a witness."

Joe's shoulders dropped. So did his smile.

"But we had anticipated this as a possibility," Joe's mom went on. "We have our witness right here with Dr. Underwood. And our hearing is set for tomorrow morning. So your arrangements to fly to Houston will have to wait."

Joe's mouth dropped. He eyed his parents. "You knew about that?"

Joe's dad nodded. "Son, I'm a police officer. Everyone in this town and in the neighboring towns knows me. So if my son is going to buy a bus ticket and a plane ticket, you'd better believe someone is going to tip me off."

Joe felt so dumb. He should've known someone would spot him and tell his dad. Sometimes it really sucked having a cop for a dad. But in this particular instance, he had no complaints.

"Sorry, Mom and Dad. I didn't think you'd let me go."

"You're right about that. We wouldn't have because she's not there. At least, not right now," his dad explained.

"Huh?"

"When I got wind of what you were doing, I decided to do my own searching. There's no trace of Infiniti Clausman in Houston, or even Texas."

Joe tightened his fist. "I knew it."

"That's why the Court is our only answer," his mom said. "If you're going to find her, you need to go to the past."

Joe couldn't believe his ears. His parents were on his side and had arranged for a meeting with the Court. That was when it hit him. They were suffering just as much as he was, maybe even more. For them to be working behind the scenes to help him like

35

that, not only with the doc but with the Court, made him feel beyond grateful. He didn't know how he could ever thank them.

"Thanks, Mom, Dad," he said bringing them in for a group hug.

For the first time in a really long time, hope soared inside of him. He was going to find Infiniti. He finally had real help and a real shot at truly finding her.

He hoped it wasn't too late.

CHAPTER 5

*P*ushing her fear of ghosts and quantum events out of her mind, Infiniti finished going through her closet and her drawers. She eyed her huge piles of clothes to donate, proud of her accomplishment. She shoved everything into garbage bags and hauled them downstairs. She plopped them by the kitchen table, then glanced at the clock. It was only six. Three more hours until her mom got home.

She hadn't eaten anything other than a few cookies at Jan's and a bag of Flamin' Hot Cheetos after that. She was ready for something more substantial. She opened the pantry, scanned her options, and settled on a bag of Ramen. Not the best or healthiest of meals, but it would do. Besides, she loved noodles.

With her dinner ready, she parked herself in front of the TV and put on a movie. Something light and funny. Finally, at nine o'clock, the back door swung open.

"Hey, Fin," her mom said.

"Hey!" Infiniti popped up from the couch, relieved to see her mom, but playing it cool. She knew her mom would roll her eyes if she mentioned her earlier conversation with Jan, so she had decided to keep it to herself.

"How was your trip?" Infiniti asked.

"The usual. Meetings, paperwork, blah, blah, blah. I'm just glad I made it home tonight. I almost missed my flight."

"Wow. I'm glad, too." Infiniti watched her mom put her stuff on the kitchen table, shuddering on the inside at the idea of almost having to sleep alone in the house with a ghost girl somewhere loose in the neighborhood. That would've sucked.

Her mom smiled, motioning at the bags of clothes. "I see you had a productive day in your closet."

"Yep, I sure did. Now I need a new wardrobe. I'll be ready to go shopping tomorrow."

Her mom laughed as she trudged her way to her room. "We'll see about that." Then she added, "I'm gonna shower and hit the hay, if that's okay. I'm beat."

"Yeah, that's fine. Goodnight."

"Goodnight, honey."

Infiniti popped some popcorn and put on another movie. She chose another light and airy comedy, still trying to erase the fear within her. By the time it ended, she could barely keep her eyes open. She turned off the lights and headed upstairs.

After a nice hot shower, she snuggled into her bed. She started drifting to sleep when she felt a presence in her room, as if someone was watching her. She cracked one eye open, not wanting to alert her intruder that she was awake, as if that would help anything. And then she thought of the creepy ghost girl she'd seen. The girl Jan had called Abigail.

Please don't let there be a ghost in my room, she thought to herself.

Ripples of panic crawled down her spine. Her heart slammed against her chest. She covered her head with her comforter, then pulled it down slowly right below her eyes. She peered about, afraid she'd see the girl, but instead spotted a tall, dark shadow of a man in the corner of her room. She opened her mouth to yell, but nothing came out.

"Listen, doll, you can't scream. You can't even run. It's just you and me, together in your dreaded nightmare."

He stepped forward. The dim light from Infiniti's alarm clock revealed a guy with short hair and a trimmed beard dressed in dark jeans and a T-shirt. Infiniti propped herself up on her elbows, thinking she could smell something burning. She studied her room, then looked back at her visitor.

"I-I-I'm dreaming?"

"That's right, doll. For now you are, and I'm here enjoying the view, waiting to claim what's mine."

She sat up even more, still smelling smoke. "Who are you?"

The guy bowed in acknowledgment. "Shade StormIron at your service, and you are Infiniti Clausman." He wagged his finger at her. "Tsk, tsk, tsk. You are quite the time traveler. You are here, you are there. It's really something keeping up with you. But my boss says I need to bring you in." He grimaced. "And I always do what my boss says."

A glow shone from under Infiniti's door. She narrowed her eyes and studied it, wondering what it was, the burning smell in her room growing stronger.

"Bring me in? Boss? What does that mean?"

Shade swooped in closer to her. He brought his face up to hers.

"It means you're dying, doll."

Infiniti's eyes snapped open.

She shot upright in bed.

Smoke filled her room. The smell of soot and ash clogged her nose and throat.

"Oh my god, oh my god," she whispered, realizing her house was on fire. Her brain somehow remembered she needed to drop to the floor, and she did. "Mom!"

She crawled to the door. She reached up and grabbed for the knob, but her hand slipped.

"Mom!"

She lunged for the knob again, catching it in a desperate hold. She turned it fast. The door swung open, and a gust of smoke rushed her room, spraying her face with heat and soot. She lay flat on the floor, pressing her cheek against the shag carpet while hacking out a series of coughs. Hot air smothered her. Tears stung her eyes. She started crawling again, military style, desperate to get downstairs to her mom's first floor room.

"Mom!"

She bumped into something in her way. She looked up and saw the tall guy from her dream. The guy that had emerged from the shadows. He was real. Smoke billowed all around him, as if he had ascended from the fiery gates of hell. Her heart slammed against her chest.

"What are you?" she choked out.

"I am a reaper." He crouched down and smiled. "You almost ready to come with me?"

Disbelief crowded her senses, followed by anger. She needed to get to her mom, and he was in the way.

"No," she squeaked out. She clenched her first, pounded at his boot, and said again, "No."

Smoke and heat filled her lungs, strangling her, forcing out a fresh spasm of coughs. She looked up at the reaper, thinking there was something oddly familiar about him, when she heard someone yelling her name.

She tried to holler back to whoever it was so they would know she was upstairs, but she couldn't speak. Her throat had shut tight.

She was dying.

She mustered all her strength to raise her arm. She swatted at the reaper, thinking to herself, *Hell no you're not taking me*, but knowing he probably would.

Everything dimmed.

Her vision tunneled.

And she plunged into darkness.

CHAPTER 6

*J*oe had prepped all night with his parents and Dr. Underwood. By morning he was as ready as he'd ever be. Facing a new day with rattled nerves and high anxiety, he studied himself in the mirror. Fresh haircut, still clean shaven from the day before. He almost looked like his old self. And with Infiniti, he'd be complete again.

His mom appeared at his door. He eyed her in the mirror.

"You sure I shouldn't wear my suit?"

He was wearing some of his old clothes since everything he had was loose. Dark jeans and black T-shirt.

She nodded. "Yes, I'm sure. If the Court approves your request, they might send you on the spot. So you need to be ready for travel."

"They'd really do that?" he asked, excited at the idea of going right away to find Infiniti, but not really believing it would happen.

"Anything is possible with the Court," she answered. "Now grab that backpack, and let's go."

"I guess it's a good thing I was planning on leaving, because now I have this backpack all ready," he joked.

She shot him a look. "Don't push it."

In the car, Joe went over everything he and his parents and the doc had discussed the night before. And when he pulled up to the parking lot of City Hall, something occurred to him. What if the Court said no? He forced that thought out of his mind, telling himself there was no way they'd say no. Especially with the doc on his side.

They entered through the secret door at the back of City Hall and descended a flight of stairs to the basement. Once at the bottom floor, they made their way down a long hallway until they came upon a reception area with a couple of chairs. Addie Beaumont was sitting in the seat closest to the hallway. She was wearing black denim pants, a plain black T-shirt, and a long dark jacket. She was the manager of the Court and pretty much knew everything going on in the town.

She peered at them from over her dark-rimmed glasses. "We just need Dr. Underwood and then—"

"I'm right here!" the doc called out, hurrying toward them.

"All right, then," Addie said to the group. She tucked her long brown hair behind her ears. "Follow me, please."

Addie went to a door on the far side of the room. She held it open. When Joe walked by her, she whispered, "Go get 'em, Joe."

Joe smiled, feeling a surge of confidence knowing he had her support, but then lost all his courage when he entered the windowless candlelit room. The place reminded him of a dungeon. A deadly dungeon. The kind of dungeon people didn't emerge from.

He followed his mom, dad, and Dr. Underwood to a long table in the middle of the room. Before him was a raised dais. The scene reminded him of the setups he'd seen on TV involving government hearings and things. Joe took a seat at the middle of the table and placed his backpack by his feet. His parents sat to his right, and Dr. Underwood filed in to the left. Joe studied the faces of the members that looked down on him. Although he knew them all, he didn't really *know them* know them, except for Sheriff Ric. He was relieved to see his pack leader up there.

Saundra Beaumont, one of the oldest witches in town, sat in the middle of the group, her silvery-white hair pulled up in a twist. She cleared her throat, silencing the murmuring in the room. She lifted a piece of paper and started to read.

"The Court of the Sun and the Moon is now in session. We are here today in the matter of a request by Joseph Greg. To wit, Joseph Greg, the petitioner, by way of his parents Katarina and Ivan Greg, with the supporting testimony of his doctor, Jasper Underwood, requests permission to time travel outside of Havenwood Falls for the purposes of locating his mate, Infiniti Clausman, a human. Said request is being sought due to the petitioner's severe and declining health. As part of the security detail of Havenwood Falls, this decline poses a serious detriment to his pack and the overall safety and security of the town. "

Joe gulped as the stately witch laid the paper down and narrowed her gaze on him.

"Does that sum it up correctly, Petitioner?"

Joe got to his feet, like his parents had instructed. "Yes." His voice cracked a little, and he felt his face flush. He swallowed and said again, "Yes. That's correct."

Saundra Beaumont studied Joe with laser focus. "Before we proceed with the hearing, I want to caution the petitioner on the seriousness of his request."

Joe felt as if every member of the Court leaned in a little. He clasped his sweaty palms behind his back, not knowing how to respond, so settled on a nod.

"Matters of time travel are fraught with danger. If you are successful here today and time travel in search of your mate, there's a possibility you will *never* return. In the event you do return, there's a possibility nothing will be the same when you get back. You might alter your life in such a way that you may never see your parents again, or this town. At least, not like you know it. Your connection to the wards may falter, and if it does, every memory of your time here will be erased. Permanently. With no chance for reversal."

The pitch of her voice grew louder with each word, and each sentence sounded almost like an argumentative plea for Joe to change his mind. As if checking herself, she paused, then added in a more controlled tone. "The risks are endless, which is why the Court would normally never entertain such a request." She folded her hands together before her. "Knowing this, are you sure you wish to proceed?"

Joe knew what he was asking. He'd gone over the severity of his request with his parents and the doc, but hearing the witch detail the perils made every hair on his body stand on edge. His gut twisted so tight it hurt. But his mind was set. Infiniti needed him, and he was going.

"Yes," he nodded. "I wish to proceed."

"And if I may add," Joe's mom said, getting to her feet. "None of us take this matter lightly. We know the dangers associated with time travel, but my husband and I cannot stand idly by while our son wastes away. The stars are aligned for good fortune and good travel. All three members of the Luna Coven's High Council are present here today. The energy in the universe supports us. I can feel it. So can my husband and our doctor. We are ready for the outcome, whatever it might be, but hold on to guarded optimism. And we do appreciate the Court's warning."

"Very well," Saundra said, looking at the Court members to her right and then to her left. "Let's get on with it, then."

Joe's mom gave him a quick squeeze before sitting back down.

Saundra shuffled her papers. "Petitioner, please explain why you seek to time travel. Why not just get on a plane and go to your mate right now?"

"Well, I was actually going to do that, except there's no trace of her today. My father can confirm that."

Joe's dad stood. "I've searched every database at my disposal. There's no record of an Infiniti Clausman anywhere in Houston or even Texas."

"Is that so?" Saundra asked.

"Yes," his dad continued. "Joe will need to find this young lady in the timeline she was returned to."

"And she's in danger," Joe blurted. "That's why I need to go to her right away."

"Hmm," Saundra said. "And what makes you think this?"

"Well," Joe explained, "when she originally left back in 2012, I had several dreams of her dying. The feelings have come back with a vengeance following her second departure this past December. Plus, the fact that she can't be located today kind of supports my theory."

"I want to hear from Dr. Underwood," Elsmed Fairchild cut in. The fae's glamour had been lowered, revealing the tips of his arrow-shaped ears. His flat nose almost touched his chin.

Joe and his dad sat while Dr. Underwood stood.

"For the record, and so it's perfectly clear, Joseph Greg has been called to Infiniti Clausman." The doc paused for a second so that the Court would understand the gravity of Joe's connection to Infiniti. "Now, I've been witnessing the decline in my patient since the departure of his mate on the eve of the Cold Moon Ball. As you all may know, he was attacked by a wild wolf pack on that evening, and I've been tending to him since then. His cracked femur has failed to heal properly, he's lost weight, and he's suffering from dehydration and tachycardia. I fear he will maintain a steady decline if not reunited with the human."

"To what end?" Elsmed asked. "Is this condition fatal?"

Dr. Underwood hesitated a moment. "It's quite possible."

Joe's stomach dropped. Hearing the doc confirm that he could be dying cemented his worst fears. Everything depended on this hearing now.

"And what if he can't find her? Or if she doesn't want to be reunited?" the fae asked in a serious and stern tone. "What of his health then, Doctor?"

"Then he'll know the truth," Dr. Underwood explained. "And can move on without her, and his health will rebound."

"Will it?" the fae pressed.

"Yes, it's my belief that it will."

A sliver of relief entered Joe, hearing that his health could rebound, but it didn't last long. He still needed the Court to rule in his favor.

"Closure," Lilith Blackstone offered. "Is that what you seek, Petitioner?"

The doc sat down while Joe got back up. He faced the petite blond-haired witch hunter he'd met once when he visited her vineyard. Her daughter, Macy, graduated a year ahead of him.

"Well, yes. If I find her, I believe she'll come back with me because she feels for me the same way that I feel for her. But if I'm wrong and she doesn't want to come with me, then I'll know and I can move on." He paused for a few seconds while the feeling of her being in danger surged inside of him. "My biggest concern, though, is getting to her before it's too late."

"Let's address this business of being too late," cut in frost dragon shifter Lawrence Mills, his white hair looking as wild as ever. Joe knew his granddaughter Zoey from school. "What does that mean exactly?"

"Well, I believe Infiniti's life is at risk, sir. It's my hope that she can come back here with me to Havenwood Falls and, um, live here in safety."

"One minute," the mage Roman Bishop said, raising his hand in a subtle yet commanding gesture, announcing to the other members he was about to speak and for them to be quiet. He was as imposing as ever with his slick black hair, tanned skin, and penetrating deep blue eyes. Joe had been told to be careful with him. "Meddling with humans bores me. Even if she is in danger, and even if one of our own is ill. I say we mind our own business."

"I agree with Roman," Old Man Mills added in his usual crotchety voice. "We should not stick our noses where they do not belong."

"Joseph Greg *is* our business, Lawrence," Saundra shot back with vigor. "I mean, look at him. His health is at risk. Can't you see that? And his true love may be in danger."

"So she comes here and then what?" Roman said between thin lips. "Where will she live? What will she do? Who will speak for her?"

Sheriff Ric rose to his feet. "I may have no vote here, but I have a voice, and my pack will speak for her. We'll speak for Joe and the entire Greg family, too, for that matter."

Joe admired Sheriff Ric already, but even more so now. He nodded at his pack leader and mouthed a quick thank you. Sheriff Ric nodded back.

"Well said, Ric," Lilith Blackstone added. "I will speak for the human, too. I am a believer in second chances. There is room at NamaStays Inn on my vineyard. She can stay there until she finds a more permanent situation."

"She can also stay with me," Saundra added, tossing Roman Bishop and Old Man Mills a look. "And I'm sure my daughter Lyra would offer the same, especially since the young lady has stayed with Lyra previously." She smiled at Joe. "I too am a believer in second chances."

"Me too," offered fae Teeny Weeny Tahini, a glittery glow shimmering about her. "I am a believer in second chances."

Joe struggled to remain calm on the outside while on the inside he was celebrating. Things were going his way!

"Fools," Roman Bishop muttered. "Meddling fools."

Old Man Mills leaned over. He eyed Roman. "Indeed," he huffed.

Joe studied the other members, wondering if they'd chime in, when Mathilde Augustine spoke.

"What of the wards? No one has mentioned them and their effect on the human."

Joe studied the powerful witch who looked like an ordinary grandmother, gathering his thoughts before he replied. He and his parents had talked about Infiniti not remembering anything and how it might be impossible to establish a connection with her again, but he had pushed that possibility aside. Failure to reach her wasn't even an option, but what if it became a reality?

He had to consider that might happen even though he didn't want to.

"I haven't forgotten about the wards. I know Infiniti won't remember me or her time here, but I still need to go. I still need to find her. And I believe—no, I *know*—I can get through to her." He clenched his jaw, his determination taking over any doubt in his mind. "I know it."

No one else said anything, and it seemed as if everyone in the room held a collective sigh of pity for Joe, but he didn't care. He was called to Infiniti, and she was connected to him, too. If he could find her, he could get through to her.

Saundra Beaumont eyed the other members of the Court, waiting to see if anyone else had any questions, when Mayor Barbie Stuart, a human, chimed in.

"Well," she said, breaking the tension in the room, "I want to make sure I'm understanding the mission of this brave young man." She had puffy blond hair and wore a low-cut top. "So the mission is to find Infiniti. Bring her back to Havenwood Falls present day if she wants to come, but leave her in her time if she wants to stay. And either outcome will restore the health of this young man, and he could possibly even be saving her life."

"Correct," Dr. Underwood said. "Thank you, Mayor, for putting it so succinctly."

With no one else speaking up, Saundra said, "Very well. Let us take it to a vote. All in favor of the Petitioner's request, raise your hand."

Everyone raised their hands except for Roman Bishop, Elsmed Fairchild, and Old Man Mills.

Saundra Beaumont banged her gavel. "With a majority, the petition passes. And in light of the decline in the petitioner's health, I recommend the petitioner be sent on his way posthaste."

Joe had been ready to celebrate when the words "posthaste" stopped him short. He shot his parents a questioning look.

"What does that mean?" he asked in a whisper.

"Now, Joseph. Posthaste means now," Saundra Beaumont

responded. She opened a box Joe hadn't noticed before and took out what looked like a small purse. "Miss Clausman's wallet was found after the thaw. We know exactly where she may be, and we are going to send you there now."

Joe couldn't believe it. He'd been searching for that wallet for months, and there it was, with the Court. And now he was being sent by the Court to find her!

His celebratory reaction was cut short when everyone started moving about with purpose. Saundra, Mathilde, Roman, and Addie gathered in the open space before Joe while the other Court members hung back. Addie waved him over. Before he went to her, Joe's mom and dad brought him in for a quick hug.

"Love you, my son," Joe's mom said in a choked voice.

"So much," his dad added.

"Love you both, too," Joe said, trying not to think of their exchange as a goodbye. "And I'll be back soon. I promise."

With a pat on his back from Dr. Underwood, Joe went to Addie and the others.

"Ground rules," Addie said. "Your tattoo prevents you from talking about the town outside the wards, as you know, but I'm gonna spell it so you can talk about it in general terms. Okay? Nothing specific."

Joe's mind scrambled with how he'd be able to talk about Havenwood Falls without really talking about it. "Okay."

"Where's your tat?" she asked.

Joe put his hand over his right bicep. "Should I take my shirt off?"

"Not necessary, I can do it through the fabric." She took a hold of his bicep and squeezed. She looked at the ground and mumbled something he couldn't make out. "There, it's done," she said, releasing him.

Saundra Beaumont approached next. "Think of the time when you want to go." She slipped a necklace around Joe's neck. "When you're ready to come back, step on the stone on this chain, and you should return to this time and this place, along with Infiniti, should she choose to come with you." She backed away and took her place in the circle. "You have seventy-two hours to accomplish your task. Before then, the stone should work. Beyond that time, it definitely will not."

"Only three days?" Joe asked.

"Longer than that would be too disruptive to the timeline," Saundra answered.

Joe's body tingled with fear and anticipation as Saundra, Mathilde, Roman, and Addie circled him. A flood of excitement mixed with trepidation soared inside of him as he watched the most powerful people in the room join hands. They started chanting, taking on expressions of concentration. The floor beneath his feet started to swirl. Slow at first, it picked up speed until it resembled a churning tornado. Joe slammed his eyes shut. He pictured Infiniti clearly in his mind. He silently repeated over and over *2013, Houston, Texas*, willing himself to go to her exactly six years in the past.

Weightlessness overcame him. His stomach turned. His body dropped into a free fall. He braced himself when his feet landed on solid ground. He opened his eyes and found himself in front of a burning house. Sparks illuminated against the dark night. Streams of black smoke wafted into the air.

"No, no, no."

Fear strangled his heart. Infiniti was inside! He knew it! And she was dying!

He started to bolt for the door when a hand jerked his arm back. Joe spun around and saw Fleet, the Transhuman who had helped Infiniti get to Havenwood Falls.

"Fleet!"

Fleet narrowed his eyes. "You know me?"

"Yes!" Joe yelled, but he knew Fleet had no memory of him. Joe shook his head. "It doesn't matter. Infiniti is in there, and she needs our help!"

Fleet studied the house for a quick second before he let go of

Joe's arm. "The fire is stronger in the rear of the home. I'll take the first floor. You go upstairs. Let's go."

Fleet ran for the door. He blasted it away with a stream of energy and disappeared inside a cloud of black smoke. Joe darted in after him. Heat stung his face and eyes. His throat and lungs clogged with deadly vapor. He dashed up the stairs, calling out for Infiniti. He didn't have to go very far when he found her sprawled out on the floor in the hallway. He scooped up her limp body and hauled her out of the house.

"Over here!" someone hollered at him.

Bystanders swarmed the area. Red lights from an ambulance and a fire truck filled the night. A paramedic ushered Joe over to a stretcher.

"Here, put her here," the man urged.

Joe laid her down gently and stepped back. He watched as the team from the ambulance descended on Infiniti's motionless form.

Fleet rushed over with a woman in his arms. Joe thought it must've been Infiniti's mom. Blackened splotches covered her face, blending in with her clothing so that Joe didn't know where skin ended and clothing began. A putrid smell filled the air. He covered his mouth and nose and turned away. Half of the team working on Infiniti broke away and started working on her mom.

Joe's head reeled. His heart shattered in a million pieces. He walked away, unable to watch Infiniti or her mom die. His vision blurred as tears filled his eyes.

"It's okay, man." Fleet said, placing his hand on Joe's back. "It's gonna be okay."

Joe's world was crashing down on him. Guilt over not acting sooner descended on him. Infiniti and her mom were dying, and it was his fault.

"I was too late," he muttered. "I got here too late."

CHAPTER 7

Fleet gave the guy some space, wondering how he knew who he was. He'd never seen the guy before. But obviously he knew Infiniti and had a deep connection with her, because he was crumbling. Fleet couldn't blame him. He knew all too well the pain of being in love with someone and having them ripped away.

The house crackled while it blazed with flames. Fire trucks blasted the inferno with streams of water. Neighbors gathered all around, either dumbstruck or crying or both. And Fleet couldn't do a damn thing. Transhumans, at least the good ones known as the Pure, didn't interfere with fate and destiny. Only the Tainted meddled in human affairs.

He moved closer to the area where the paramedics were working on Infiniti and her mom. They were being strapped into place for transport. Oxygen masks covered their faces. Fleet eyed their chests, looking for movement, hoping they were alive, but the bustling about of the paramedics obstructed his view.

"Looks like you and the Havenwoodie were just a little too late, cupcake."

Fleet spun around and saw Shade StormIron. His arms were crossed as he leaned against the ambulance. Of all the reapers he'd encountered over the years, Shade irritated him the most. Fleet clenched his fists at his side.

"You son of a bitch."

"Yep, I'm that, and other things. And as much as I'd love to sit here and chat with your moody self, I need to catch my ride."

The reaper dissolved into a stream of black and filtered into the ambulance as it drove off.

"Dammit," Fleet muttered, wondering whose life the reaper was going to claim, thinking the mom for sure but uncertain about Infiniti.

He stood in the middle of the street, angry as hell, determined to do whatever he could to help Tiny and her mom. He stomped over to the guy the reaper had referred to as a Havenwoodie, wondering why someone from Havenwood Falls would be in Houston with Infiniti, but starting to piece things together. Everything had to do with Abigail's cryptic message.

"Hey, man, what's your name?"

The guy wiped his face with his shirt sleeve while he pulled himself together. "Joe. My name is Joe."

"Okay, Joe. Come on. We're following that ambulance."

They got into Fleet's car down the street and sped up to the ambulance. The lights were blinking; the siren was blaring. Fleet knew the display wasn't a good sign. After about ten minutes of driving, they arrived at a hospital. Fleet parked in the nearest spot, and he and Joe hurried over to the emergency entrance.

A team of doctors and nurses dashed out of the building. They stood behind the ambulance while the doors opened. A stretcher with a body covered in a sheet came out first.

Fleet halted. So did Joe. Time stood still for a few seconds until Infiniti came out in the second stretcher.

"Damn," Fleet mumbled. Even though a part of him was happy to see that Infiniti had made it, he didn't want anyone to die. He knew Infiniti would be devastated. She and her mom were close, and she was the only family Infiniti had.

The stretchers disappeared inside the hospital. Fleet and Joe were about to follow them in when one of the paramedics spotted them.

"Hey, the guys from the fire. Y'all okay?"

Not knowing anything about Joe, Fleet thought being seen by a doc might do him good. Even though he wasn't in the house long, Fleet suspected he'd taken in a lot of smoke. Plus, they'd be closer to Tiny.

"We're no worse for wear, but could use a once over. And hey, I'm sorry the mom didn't make it."

"Us too," the guy said, shaking his head. "We did everything we could. Losing someone never gets easier."

"And Infiniti? The girl?" Joe asked. "She's gonna be okay?"

"I'm pretty sure she is." The paramedic led them to the hospital entrance and called one of the nurses over. "It's a good thing you two were around. A few more minutes and she would've ended up like her mom."

A nurse with a clipboard put Fleet and Joe in a room. She started Joe on oxygen right away. She handed a mask to Fleet, but he held up his hand.

"I'm fine."

The nurse eyed him. "Suit yourself."

"So, Infiniti is okay?" Joe asked her. "The paramedic said she was, but is she really?"

"The young lady? Yes, I believe so," the nurse said.

"Can I see her?"

Fleet thought Joe would come unglued if he couldn't see her soon.

"Are you family?" the nurse asked.

"No, but she's very special to me."

"I'll see what I can do, but let me get your information first." She took out a pen from her pocket and handed it over with clipboard.

"I can fill those out," Fleet said.

"You two related?"

"Yes," Fleet said. "We are." He was a pro at filling out forms with the go-to fake information he and his brother had used for years.

"Okay, then," the nurse said. "You fill those out, and I'll be back with a doctor as soon as one is available. It's a busy night, so it may be a while." She nodded at Joe. "I'll see what I can do about that visit."

Alone now, Fleet moved his chair in front of Joe's. He leaned over, resting his elbows on his knees.

"Okay, let's hear it. How do you know me, and what's the situation with you and Tiny?"

Joe took off his mask. "That's right, you call Infiniti Tiny."

"Yeah, I do. Now spill."

"Well, I'm Joe, like I said, and I know you and Infiniti from the future, where I'm from." Joe paused, as if waiting for Fleet to react, but he held a steady expression. He'd done enough time traveling and had lived enough lives to know anything was possible.

"I'm from H—" He stopped, looking dumbfounded, as if he'd forgotten what he was going to say. "I'm from H-H-H, argh, I can't say it."

Fleet raised a brow. He knew exactly where the guy was from. Shade had called him a Havenwoodie, and Abigail had mentioned Havenwood Falls. Fleet figured the guy was from there but couldn't talk about it because of the town enchantment Abigail had mentioned.

"You're from Havenwood Falls," Fleet said.

"Yes!" Joe said, blowing out with relief. "You and Infiniti came to town in December 2018. Actually, she first arrived December 2012."

Fleet sat back and crossed his arms, absorbing the information. "That makes no sense."

Joe ran his fingers through his hair. "Infiniti was in a car crash that happened outside of town in December 2012. She was brought to the medical center. She disappeared, but then reappeared in December 2018. And when she reappeared, you were with her."

Joe paused to see if Fleet had any questions, but he didn't. Not yet anyway.

"We figured out she needed something from my time—a spell to make her a void so harmful magic couldn't hurt her. The spell was performed, and then the two of you left and came back here to your proper time to help someone named Dominique. You guys don't remember any of it because of the protective wards around the town that wipes everyone's memories of their visit when they leave."

Fleet rubbed the back of his neck. "Then how do you remember all this? We're not in Havenwood Falls."

Joe shifted in his seat. He stitched his brows together. "The memories fade over time, but I just got here. That's how I still remember. But I've also been released from some of the magic of the wards so that I can say a few things about where I'm from. And I only have seventy-two hours."

"Seventy-two hours for what?"

"To get back home with Infiniti."

Fleet got up and started pacing the room, analyzing Joe's words. So Abigail was right. He had been to Havenwood Falls with Infiniti to help her find a spell. And now he had helped save her from a fire. But to what end?

"Hey, did everything work out with that Dominique person?" Joe asked.

Fleet stopped in his tracks. The story of Dominique's final life and everything he, Farrell, Dominique, Trent, and Infiniti had been through was long and complicated. He didn't think Joe needed all the gory and gut-wrenching details.

"For some it has."

Fleet continued pacing. He still didn't know why Joe was here.

"So why come back? Why risk traveling from your time to this time? Why are you—?" Fleet stopped mid-sentence because he knew the answer. It was love. Love made people do dumb-ass things.

"You're in love with Infiniti."

Joe rubbed his hands on his jeans. "Yes, but it's way more than that. I'm a wolf shifter, and I'm called to her. She's my mate. For life. During our time together, she developed strong feelings for me, too. When she left, she made me promise to find her." He looked away for a few long seconds. "I've been trying to make good on that promise since December, hoping I could find her and bring her back with me. Not only because of my connection to her and my failing health since she's been gone, but also because I kept feeling like she was in danger here." He lowered his head. "And she was."

When Joe finished his story, Fleet saw him in a different light. Gaunt face, tired eyes. Through the soot and ash on his face and body, Fleet could see the guy was wasting away from heartache. Plus, he was right. He had saved Infiniti. In light of Abigail's message, Fleet thought her life was still at risk, but didn't want to say so unless he knew for certain.

"What if Infiniti doesn't believe your story? What if you can't get through to her? Or what if she doesn't want to go with you?"

"I have three days to try my best. Assuming the worst case scenario and things don't go my way, I return home. My doc thinks my health will rebound because at least I would have tried."

The theory made sense to Fleet. Getting over a heartache was much easier when the affection was one-sided. "Okay, fine. So why do you need me then?"

"I don't know," Joe said. "I guess we still need to figure that part out."

Fleet and Joe fell into a lull of silence. After about an hour, they decided it was best to not see the doctor after all and told the nurse they'd be in the waiting room, hoping to see Infiniti.

They stayed in the overcrowded room all night. Sitting in the corner as far away as possible from the coughing and sneezing people in the cramped space, they spent their time analyzing their situation. And while the minutes ticked by, Fleet kept wondering how Infiniti would react when she finally saw him and Joe. Would she remember all the crap they'd been through during their ordeal with Dominique? Would she see Joe and remember her feelings for him? And was she still in danger?

He had no idea, but sooner or later they were going to come face to face with her and find out.

CHAPTER 8

Something felt stuck in Infiniti's throat. Like a piece of food—a noodle or something. She'd eaten ramen for dinner, so thought maybe that was it. With her eyes closed, she reached over to her bedside table for the water bottle she kept there. That's when a flood of awareness washed over her.

She remembered smoke and fire. She could practically feel the heat from the flames, could taste the soot in her nose and throat. She jolted upright in bed. Tingles of fear raced over her body. Her breathing came out in panic-filled bursts.

Fire! Her house was on fire!

"Mom!" she shouted in a hoarse voice, her airway throbbing with pain.

"Shh, Infiniti. It's okay."

It took Infiniti a few seconds to see Jan standing next to her, holding her hand. Tears filled her neighbor's eyes.

"I'm right here, dear. I'm right here."

Infiniti struggled to speak, not even knowing what to ask. She eyed her surroundings and found herself in a hospital room. An IV was attached to her arm. Her hands patted their way up her chest and to her nose, where plastic prongs nestled in her nostrils.

Her breathing steadied, but not by much. "W-w-what happened? W-w-where's my mom?"

Jan looked down while Infiniti's heart pounded out of control. Shivers rippled up and down her body as she waited for her neighbor to speak.

"My dear, your house caught on fire. You and your mother were pulled out and brought to the hospital by ambulance. You've suffered moderate smoke inhalation, but," Jan's voice choked up, "your mother's smoke inhalation was severe." Jan struggled to silence her sobs. "And . . . she didn't make it."

Infiniti stared at Jan, wide-eyed, struggling to make sense of her words as they swirled in her head like a foggy storm. Tears welled up in her eyes.

"What? She didn't make . . . what?"

Deep down, Infiniti knew what Jan meant, but needed to hear the words. It wasn't real without the words.

"She didn't survive. She passed away in the ambulance."

Infiniti's heart shattered into a billion pieces. Her body shook uncontrollably. A flood of tears gushed out of her. She clutched Jan and held her tight, letting every tear spill out of her as she tried to make sense of what had happened.

She had lost her mom, the only person in the world she had. Infiniti didn't want to stop crying, didn't want to let go of Jan, but someone opened the door of her room.

"Ladies, my apologies, but I have some questions for Miss Clausman."

Infiniti looked up and saw a portly white-haired police officer with a full beard.

Jan huffed. "Officer, please! Can't this wait? The fire just happened tonight! Give us some time!"

He came in all the way and shut the door behind him. "It can't. My apologies again. I have a few questions while everything is fresh in mind. It's procedure."

Infiniti pulled her hospital sheet up to her face and wiped her cheeks. "It's okay," she said to Jan. "I-I-I think I can do it."

"Okay," Jan said, moving to the other side of the bed, giving the officer room for his questioning. "I'll be right here, and if you want to stop, you let me know," she said to Infiniti. She directed a scowl at the officer. "You have two minutes, Officer."

The officer cleared his throat. "I'm very sorry about your loss, young lady. I promise to make this as short and painless as possible." He took a small pad and pencil out of his shirt pocket. "Tell me everything you can about the fire. Anything you remember."

Infiniti thought back to her evening. "Well, my mom came home from a business trip. She put her stuff on the kitchen table and then went straight to bed. I stayed up and popped some popcorn and watched a movie. When it was over, I showered and went to bed too. And then I woke up because I smelled smoke."

"So everything was normal? Nothing out of the ordinary?"

Icy fear coursed through Infiniti's veins when suddenly she remembered a dream she was having right before she woke up.

"I was having a nightmare," she half whispered.

The officer gave Infiniti a curious look. He moved in closer. "A nightmare?"

Infiniti's head pounded with pain, but she forced herself to recall the dream. "I dreamed there was a guy in my room. He told me I was dying. And then, when I woke up, I saw him."

The officer stopped his note taking. "There was an intruder in your house?"

"No, I mean, yes, I mean . . . he was a reaper."

The officer looked from Infiniti to Jan back to Infiniti. "Miss Clausman, was there a person in your house? I'm not talking about dreams or make-believe creatures. Was there a real live person in your residence?"

"If she said it, then she saw it!" Jan declared, coming to Infiniti's defense.

Infiniti's lip started quivering. She knew what she had seen. But she also knew how it sounded. A reaper from her dreams actually appearing before her? Who would believe that? She glanced at Jan, grateful for her neighbor's support, but second-guessed herself. Maybe the smoke had caused her to hallucinate. Maybe she hadn't really seen what she thought she had. Maybe losing her mother was making her crazy.

She rubbed her forehead. "I don't know. There was a reaper in my dream. And then I thought I saw him. But I must've been imagining it, because reapers don't exist, right?" She eyed Jan. "Right? They don't exist?"

Jan placed a reassuring hand on Infiniti's shoulder. "They do not, dear."

Infiniti stared up and away, picturing the reaper clearly in her mind. And then she remembered the smoke. "There was smoke everywhere."

"There was smoke everywhere and then what?" the officer asked, glazing over the reaper part, dismissing it entirely.

"I fell to the ground like you're supposed to do in a fire, and crawled out of my room trying to get to my mom. I made it into the hallway and . . ." She could still see the reaper's boots before her, could see his face and hear his words, but she didn't say so. "And I couldn't breathe and I guess I passed out."

"And it was only you and your mom in the house, correct?"

"Yes." Fresh tears spilled out of her. "It was just the two of us. It was always just the two of us."

Jan cut in with a curt tone. "Elizabeth Clausman was a single mother. She had no husband and no other family. Is that enough for now?"

The officer turned his attention to Jan. "Yes, ma'am. Thank you. And you are?"

"My name is Jan Kelly. I live across the street from Infiniti. I've known Infiniti her entire life. She and her mother are family to me."

He handed Jan the notebook. "Please put down your name, address, and contact numbers in case I need to reach you."

Jan jotted down the information and handed the notebook back to the officer. He closed it up and put it back in his pocket.

"That's all I need right now. Thank you both very much. I'll be in touch should I need anything further. And my sincerest condolences."

When he left the room, Infiniti pulled Jan's arm, desperate to talk about what she had seen.

"There really was a reaper. He said his name was Shade StormIron. He said his boss wanted me."

Jan placed her hands on Infiniti's shoulders. She helped her ease back into the bed. "Dear, I believe you. I really do. But it's three in the morning, and you need some sleep. We can talk more after you've rested."

Infiniti let herself fall back onto her pillow, but couldn't relax. Her neck and shoulders were stiff and tight. A sick feeling had sunk so far down in her stomach she could barely breathe.

"Where's . . . my mom?" she asked in a hushed tone.

"She's here, in the hospital. Being prepared for the next step in her journey."

Infiniti had talked with her mom about death and dying and knew she wanted to be cremated. But the idea of handling all that was too much for her.

"Jan, I can't be the one to make any decisions about—"

"I'll see to it, dear. I know what your mother wanted. I'll make all the arrangements."

Infiniti nodded.

"I'll let you rest now."

Another nod.

Before Jan could say anything else, Infiniti popped up. "How did I get out of my house?"

"A young man ran in and carried you out. Another young man carried your mom. Now sleep. It's late, and a new day will be here soon."

Fear clenched Infiniti's insides as Jan turned off the light and rested her hand on the door.

"You're leaving?"

"Only to secure my house, look in on Tinker, and gather some

things we'll be needing. And then I'll be right back. I promise."
She pointed at a chair in the corner. "I'll be snoozing right there
with you before you know it."

Infiniti didn't want Jan to leave. She was terrified of being
alone, but understood why Jan needed to go.

"Okay. Just hurry, please."

"I will."

Infiniti rested her head back down, watching as the door
slowly swung shut. A steady stream of tears rolled down her face
and onto her pillow. She decided to forget about the reaper, telling
herself he wasn't real as she cried herself to sleep.

Infiniti's eyes flitted open when she heard someone rustling about
in her room. After a quick moment of fear, she saw her nurse
standing beside her.

"I'm checking your vitals," she said with a smile. "I didn't
mean to startle you."

Disoriented, Infiniti let the nurse do what she needed to do as
she scanned her room. She studied the hazy glow of early morning
sunlight peeking through her blinds.

"What time is it?" Infiniti muttered.

"It's five thirty in the morning," the nurse answered, then left
the room.

Infiniti's gaze went to the chair, and sure enough, there was
Jan, head pressed against a pillow that had been propped against
the wall. Her shoulders eased when she saw her neighbor, and she
lay back down. She thought of everything that had happened,
playing the evening over and over in her mind on repeat until Jan
stirred, her bones creaking and popping as she shifted.

"Jan?" Infiniti asked. "Are you awake?"

"Yes, I am," Jan answered, rubbing her leg. She sat up all the
way, moving her pillow to the floor. "Did you sleep okay?"

"No. Did you?"

"Not really." Jan smiled.

The stink of smoke and soot still permeated Infiniti, and she needed to get rid of it. "I could use a shower," she said to Jan.

"Good," Jan said. "Let me get a nurse to unhook you from your contraptions."

Infiniti sat in a daze while the nurse came back in and started working on her. Once she was free of the oxygen and the saline bag, both of which the nurse said she didn't need anymore, she took a long hot shower. She washed away the residue from her ordeal, but couldn't do anything about the pain in her heart.

What was her life going to be like now? Where would she live? What would she do?

After her shower, she dressed in new clothes Jan had purchased for her and started nibbling on the hospital breakfast. A knock sounded on the door, and a woman dressed in a business suit came in.

"Miss Clausman, my name is Jessica Ramirez. I'm the hospital administrator. I have a few things to go over with you about your mother—things Ms. Kelly and I went over last night while you were asleep."

Infiniti pushed her food away while her gut clenched and a new supply of tears welled up in her eyes.

The woman had light brown hair and a kind smile. She handed Infiniti a box of tissues, pulled up a chair, and sat down. "I know this is difficult, and I'm glad you have your neighbor here to help you. These conversations are not easy, but we need to discuss arrangements for your mother. I'd like for you to confirm what Ms. Kelly has authorized."

The woman opened her notebook. "Ms. Kelly has arranged for a funeral home to retrieve the body and make preparations for cremation. As the only surviving relative, can you confirm that's what your mother wanted?"

"Yes," Infiniti said in a hoarse whisper. "That's what she wanted."

"Once the body leaves the possession of the hospital, we will require no further documentation besides financial settlement for our services." The woman handed Infiniti a piece of paper. "This details what I've just explained. If you can please sign at the bottom." Infiniti took a pen from the woman and signed her name. "And this is for your records," the woman concluded. She handed Infiniti a set of the papers she had just signed. "The official death certificate should be ready in about two weeks."

Infiniti blinked as those words sunk in.

"Anything else?" Jan asked.

"The doctor has cleared Miss Clausman for release. However, you can stay here another night if you feel observation is necessary. It's up to you."

"I want to leave today and go . . ." Infiniti's voice trailed off because she had no idea where she would go.

"My house," Jan offered. "Infiniti will come to my house."

"Very well," the woman said. She got up to leave. "Once again, on behalf of the hospital, we offer our sincere condolences."

Infiniti eyed the paperwork, feeling sick to her stomach. "People get certificates for dying? Like, good job, here's your certificate?"

Jan took the papers and stuffed them in her oversized bag. "I never thought of it that way, but you're right. It's a ridiculous thing to call it."

The door opened again. A nurse Infiniti hadn't seen yet entered the room.

"Pardon my interruption, but the two young men from the fire last night are still in the waiting room. They would like to see you."

Infiniti wiped her eyes with a tissue. She sat up. "The ones who carried me and my mom out of my house?"

"Yes. They didn't want to leave without seeing you."

Infiniti wondered who had run into her burning house. Who would risk their lives like that?

"Well, I guess I should thank them." She turned to Jan. "Right? I should see them and thank them?"

"It's up to you, but it would be a nice gesture."

It had to have taken a lot of courage and bravery to run into a flaming house for a stranger. The least she could do was see her rescuers.

"They risked their lives for me and my mom. So yes, I'd like to thank them," she said to the nurse.

"I'll bring them up, then."

The nurse left as another person came in with even more check-out paperwork. Infiniti was glad for all the interruptions. It kept her mind off the horror of her situation. Jan went outside with the woman, leaving Infiniti alone. Not a minute later, the phone by her bed rang, startling her. She answered the call.

"Hello?"

"Fin! It's Trent!"

A fresh flood of tears rushed to her eyes, clogging her throat and strangling her words. Trent was her best friend in the whole world. He'd left for college a few weeks earlier.

"Fin, are you there?"

"Yes," she squeaked out, but couldn't fight the tears anymore. "Trent," she said between blubbering sobs. "My house caught on fire, and my mom—"

Pain and heartache wrestled her so tight she couldn't get the words out.

"I know, Fin," he said in a low voice. "I know. I'm so sorry. I saw the news. I've been trying to reach you for hours."

The last time she had used her phone was in her bedroom before she went to bed. For all she knew, it had burned to a crisp. "I don't have a phone anymore," she sobbed. "I don't have anything anymore."

"I can't get to you for few days, but I'm coming. Okay? I'll be there."

She wiped her tears away. "Okay."

"Where will you be?"

"Jan's."

"Okay, I'll be there, Fin. Everything will be okay. You just hold on."

"Okay."

She hung up and dragged herself over to the bathroom. She splashed cold water on her face, thinking she'd never get over losing her mother. She was back on her bed, feeling completely drained, when her door cracked open.

"Miss Clausman, I have your visitors, if you're ready."

She wasn't ready at all, but wanted to thank the guys who had rushed into her house. It was the least she could do.

"All right," she said, smoothing out her crisp new shirt. "I'm ready."

The nurse opened the door all the way and in walked two guys —a tall slender one with short blond hair and hazel green eyes and another guy who was even taller with short dark hair and a trimmed beard. Ash residue stained their shirts and jeans. Taking them in, she thought she'd seen them before, especially the blond guy. Something about him reminded her of someone she knew, though she couldn't figure out who.

"Here are the young men, Miss Clausman," the nurse said with a nod before leaving the three of them alone.

Infiniti tucked her hair behind her ears. It was still damp from her shower. "So, you're the ones who ran into my house?"

The guy with dark hair dropped to the back while the slender guy with blond hair moved forward. "Yes, we did. I'm Joe, and this is Fleet. We wanted to check on you and make sure you were okay. We're very sorry about your mom."

A surge of recognition tugged at her, as if she recognized his voice.

"Thank you," she said after a long pause. Her eyes watered over again, but this time she managed to stop the flow. She looked away from her visitors, embarrassed for them to see her like this.

"I'm so sorry," she said, dabbing at her eyes with a tissue. "I can't seem to stop crying."

"It's okay, Infiniti," Joe said, getting closer. "You don't have to apologize."

Staring into his beautiful face, she thought he was looking at her as if he'd known her forever. As if he really and truly cared about her.

"Do I know you?' she asked. "Have we met?"

"I'll leave you two alone," the dark-haired guy said. "I'll be right outside, Joe."

Infiniti didn't pay him any attention as he left. She couldn't keep her eyes off Joe.

He stuffed his hands in his jeans pocket. "I've seen you around, but we haven't exactly met."

"Oh," she said. "I guess that must be it then, because you seem so familiar to me."

"Yeah." He smiled. "That must be it."

A long silence grew between them while Infiniti thought of her usual hangouts where she might've run into Joe but couldn't pinpoint him at any particular place.

"So," she said. "I guess you were by my house when it caught on fire?"

"Um, yeah, I was. Fleet came up, and we ran in together."

She pointed her finger at the door. "Fleet came up to you? So he wasn't with you?"

"No, we kind of saw each other on the sidewalk and then teamed up together."

"So you don't know him?"

Joe hesitated for a few seconds. "I know him, but not that well."

"Oh," Infiniti said, trying to make sense of it all.

Jan waltzed back in, nearly bumping into Joe.

"My apologies," she said. "I didn't know you had company, dear."

"This is Joe. He's one of the guys that came into the house for me and mom."

Joe held out his hand for a shake. "I'm Joseph Greg. Nice to meet you, ma'am."

"I'm Jan Kelly. Thank you so much for your bravery and heroism. The world needs more young men like you."

The name Joseph Greg sparked a recognition deep within Infiniti. She knew, without a doubt, she'd heard his name before. But from where?

She tilted her head. "Your name is Joseph Greg?"

"Yes," he said, his eyes lighting up. "Do you recognize my name?"

"I think so, but I'm not sure. Maybe you just have one of those names."

"Maybe I do," he said, looking a little defeated, but still holding a hopeful look on his face.

"Infiniti," Jan said, interrupting them. "We can leave now. I've taken care of all the paperwork."

Infiniti swung her legs to get out of bed. Joe extended his hand to help her up, and when she put her hand in his, a weakness struck her knees. A flurry of butterflies exploded in her stomach. She looked up at him, wondering if he felt what she had, but didn't want to ask. She had lost her mom and had almost lost her own life, and here she was having feelings for her rescuer? It was the worst timing ever, but she couldn't help herself.

A nurse entered the room with a wheelchair.

"I have to go now," she said, suddenly not wanting to leave him. "I'll be going to Jan's house. She lives across the street from me." She paused, feeling crazy for asking him to come over but overcome with the need to see him again. "In case you maybe, I don't know, want to check on me or something."

"Yeah," he said. "Sure. I'd like that, if that's okay."

"Yeah, that would be okay. Thank you again, Joe. And tell your friend Fleet I said thank you."

"Of course," he said. "I will." And then he added before she left, "I'm really glad you're okay, Infiniti. Really, really glad."

She tilted her head a little at him, thinking there was

something about him that was comforting and lovable. She mustered a weak smile. "Me too."

Infiniti eased herself onto the wheelchair. The nurse rolled her out of the room, and Jan walked by her side. Her thoughts flooded with competing feelings—grief over losing her mother and a deep connection to Joe. She pushed it aside, not able to deal with the warring emotions, when the wheelchair stopped at the elevator bank. Infiniti's gaze landed on a nearby bulletin board. She spotted a piece of paper with thick black lettering. She peered closer.

Infiniti,
I'm coming for you.
Death

Infiniti gasped. She grasped Jan's arm.

"What is it?" Jan asked. "Are you okay?"

Infiniti glanced at Jan, then pointed at the note, but the message was gone. Instead, the note contained an ad about a nearby sandwich shop. She shook her head.

"I thought I saw—" The elevator door opened with a ding, and Infiniti scooted the wheelchair forward with her legs.

"Miss, are you okay?" the young nurse asked, helping Infiniti get into the elevator with a gentle push on the wheelchair.

"Yes," she said, slapping the button for the first floor. "I just want to get out of here."

"Infiniti?" Jan asked. "What in the world?"

"Please, Jan. Let's just go," she whispered, pinching the bridge of her nose and telling herself her eyes must've been playing tricks on her. Just like they did back in her room with that reaper.

Once in the car, she and Jan drove in silence. As they got closer to their neighborhood, Jan started warning Infiniti about the condition of her house. But when they rolled down the street, nothing could've prepared her for the horrific sight of her childhood home.

She covered her mouth with her hand.

"Oh my god," she uttered between her fingers.

The scene reminded Infiniti of something she might see in a

war movie. Windows were busted out. The front door and entry looked as if it had been blasted by a bomb. Streaks of char covered the left side of the house, spreading across the first floor and reaching up into the second. Yellow caution tape circled the premises. She didn't feel the tears streaming down her face until Jan handed her a fresh tissue.

All of her things were ruined. The memories of her childhood altered forever in the most horrendous way. She knew she'd never be the same after this.

CHAPTER 9

*J*oe wanted nothing more than to hug Infiniti, cradle her in his arms, kiss her, and tell her everything was going to be okay, but he couldn't. She didn't know him. To her, he was a stranger who'd run into her home and carried her out. Yet despite that, he could tell something about him seemed familiar to her. He replayed their conversation in his mind, wondering if he should've said more, but he knew it would've been too much for her. She was crushed from the loss of her mother.

"What happened?" Fleet asked, coming into the room.

"She remembered something when I touched her hand. There was a spark in her eyes. She even thought my name sounded familiar."

Fleet crossed his arms. "That's a good sign. Now what?"

"She told me where she was staying. Even said I could go check on her."

Fleet patted his back. "Okay. So all you need to do is go over there and get through to her."

Joe glanced at the clock on the wall. His time was ticking, and even though he didn't want to be too pushy, he realized Fleet was right. He needed to go to her and right away. Especially since he still felt as if she could be in danger.

"What is it?" Fleet asked. "You've got a look."

Joe rubbed the back of his neck. "I can't shake the feeling that something horrible is going to happen to her."

"Still? More than the fire?"

"Yes."

"All right then," Fleet said. "Let's regroup, but not here. I saw a shopping center down the way and a motel. We could both use a shower and a fresh change of clothes. Come on."

"Good idea," Joe said. And then he remembered the backpack he'd left back in the Court chambers.

"Uh," he said. "I have no money."

"I've got it. Don't worry."

After making a quick stop for new clothes, they grabbed some burgers and drinks and got a motel room not far from Infiniti's house. The beige-on-beige room with two double beds promised a hot shower and a place for them to strategize.

"I'll go first," Fleet said, disappearing into the bathroom.

Joe eyed the pillow. He hadn't slept hardly at all in the hospital waiting room and could use a quick rest. He eased himself onto the bed. His fatigued body ached all over. Even his limp felt worse, as if his bones were revolting against him. He stared at the popcorn-textured ceiling and thought of Infiniti. He had to get through to her before something else happened and before his time was up, and then he could smash the stone on the necklace Sandra Beaumont had given him and he and Infiniti could go back home. She'd be safe back there.

"It's gonna work out," he whispered to himself. "It has to."

He thought about the necklace. Everything had been happening so fast, he hadn't had time to even look at it. He reached for it, but didn't feel it around his neck. He jolted upright. He patted his shirt up at the front near the collar, then all the way to the back. He dropped to the floor, looking all around the carpet. He took Fleet's keys and hurried to the car parked outside their room. He searched every nook and cranny, but it wasn't there either.

He trudged himself back to the room. He pressed his palms against the wall. How were he and Infiniti going to get back to Havenwood Falls and 2019 now? Frustration starting building inside of him. How could he have lost the one thing he really needed? Seething with anger at himself and his messed up situation, he slammed his fist into the wall.

Fleet came out of the restroom. "Whoa. What's up with you?"

Joe pulled his hand out of the sheetrock. He rubbed his knuckles. "I lost it."

"I can see that." Dressed in new jeans and a T-shirt, Fleet toweled off his wet hair. "Or did you actually lose something?"

Joe blew out. "I punched the wall because I lost mine and Infiniti's ticket back home to H-H-H." Joe growled, wanting to punch his other hand through the wall, pissed that he couldn't talk about his home.

"Havenwood Falls," Fleet said, completing the sentence.

"Right. I lost our way to get back there."

Fleet raised an eyebrow. "What do you mean?"

"I was given a necklace with a stone that I was supposed to use to take me and Infiniti back to where I'm from." He kicked at the wall. "And I lost it."

Fleet sat on a wooden chair by the window of the room. "Well, maybe that's why I'm here. Maybe I'm your way back."

Hope filtered into Joe. "That's right. I've seen you in action. You can do your thing and get us home."

"You've seen me in action?" Fleet asked, looking doubtful.

"Yeah, back in H-H-H—my home. I saw the stream of energy pouring out of your hands. It swirled around the room until you and Infiniti vanished into it."

Fleet tossed his towel on the bed. "Sounds about right."

Joe faced Fleet, thinking of his Transhuman skills. "It'll work, right? You can do it again?"

"Of course it'll work. Now go shower. We've got shit to do."

Joe hobbled his way to the bathroom. He turned the water as hot as he could and let it pummel his worn-out body. He watched as dark residue pooled around his feet from the ash and soot he'd been carrying for hours. He thought of all the things Infiniti had lost in the fire, including her mother. It seemed like the odds were stacked against them. He wondered if the tides would ever turn their way.

Standing in the hot stream, Joe resigned to trust Fleet's ability to send them home. All he needed to do was get through to Infiniti. He lathered up the soap while racking his brain with ways to see Infiniti again when flowers popped into his mind. He could take her some flowers and maybe she'd invite him inside and they could chat. But then what? How could he even begin to tell her that he was from the future and that they had fallen in love when she had transported there? And that he thought she was in danger and should go back with him? Not to mention the whole wolf shifter thing. He leaned his forehead against the shower tile and groaned.

Why couldn't anything be easy?

He finished up in a hurry, got dressed, and joined Fleet in the main room. Fleet pointed at his leg.

"What happened to you?"

Joe rubbed his thigh. "Funny you should ask, because you were there when this happened. I was attacked by a pack of wild wolves. I would've been much worse off if you hadn't shown up when you did."

"Why didn't you heal up? You are a wolf shifter, right? Aren't you supposed to heal fast?"

"I am, and the break should've healed long ago, but this whole thing with Infiniti has me messed up."

Fleet rubbed his chin. He eyed Joe's leg. "Want me to take a crack at it?"

There was a lot Joe didn't know about Transhumans, but if Fleet could fix his leg, then he was all in.

"Sure. I'd love to be able to walk without an old-man limp."

Fleet motioned for Joe to sit on the edge of the bed. He scooted the chair over and sat in front of him. He narrowed his eyes while he hovered his hands over Joe's leg. He moved them up and down, then stopped midway between the hip and knee.

"There it is," Fleet said. "Hold on."

Fleet closed his eyes. He placed his fingers on the spot. His hands started to glow, reminding Joe of how Dr. Underwood had tried to heal him. The light from Fleet's hands intensified until a gray mist started trickling out of his palms. Fleet grimaced, and a crackle of electricity shot out of his hands. Joe's leg spasmed.

"This is deep," Fleet said between gritted teeth. He held his touch a few more seconds before he dropped his hands.

Joe rubbed his leg. "Did it work?"

"Not completely, but you should be able to walk better."

Joe got up and walked around the room. His limp wasn't completely gone, but it was much better. "This is good. Thanks, Fleet."

Joe continued moving about the room. "So I've got an idea about Infiniti. She told me she was staying with her neighbor across the street. The lady from the hospital. What do you think if I went to see her with some flowers? Maybe she'd invite me in, and I could, you know, try to get through to her."

"That's not a bad idea. While you're visiting, I can sift through the rubble of her house and look for your necklace."

A twinge of worry struck Joe. "I thought you said we didn't need it."

"Just in case."

Those three words stayed with Joe while he and Fleet went to a nearby florist and then to Infiniti's. The idea of needing a "just in case" option set his nerves on edge and soared within him as they drove to Infiniti's house. And when they parked in front of the burnt remains of her home, Joe couldn't believe his eyes.

"Damn." Fleet whistled.

"We ran into that," Joe gulped.

Seeing the destruction made him realize how lucky he was that he found Infiniti so quickly and got her out before it was too late. And even though he could've died, he'd do it all over again. His gaze went to the house across the street where Infiniti was staying. He hoped she was okay.

"Come on," Joe prompted, eager and nervous all at the same time. "Let's see if she's there."

He approached Jan's house first while Fleet hung back a little. He rang the doorbell. After a few long seconds, Infiniti opened the door.

"Hi," Joe said awkwardly, trying not to be too excited. With everything she'd been through, he needed to play it cool.

"Hi," she said with a fragile smile.

Her eyes were puffy from crying, and the tip of her petite nose was red, but she was still the most beautiful girl he'd ever seen.

She motioned at the flowers. "Are those for me?"

"Oh, yeah, here." He handed her the flowers he'd almost forgotten he was holding.

"Thank you, Joe. They're beautiful."

Joe had no idea what to say next, but luckily Fleet saved him. "Joe wanted to make sure you were okay." Fleet pointed his thumb over his shoulder at Infiniti's house behind him. "And if you don't mind, could I check your yard for a necklace Joe lost?"

She eyed her house with the saddest look Joe had ever seen.

"Sure," she said to Fleet. "Go ahead."

Fleet left them, and Joe searched for what to say next.

"So, you're doing okay?"

She shrugged her shoulders. "I guess I'm okay."

"Good," he said. "I'm glad."

A few more awkward moments of silence set in.

"Do you want to come in?"

"That would be great," he said, relieved.

He followed her to the kitchen and watched as she got a vase from under the sink. She put the flowers in it and started filling it with water.

"Are you by yourself?" he asked, looking around the room.

"Yeah, Jan left not too long ago for the store."

Joe studied the traditional kitchen with dark-grained cabinets and white laminate counters. He thought everything looked a little dated, especially now that most people had granite countertops. He still remembered when his own kitchen back home was updated. It was the first time he thought of being in a different time, and he instantly thought of his family. He hoped they weren't too worried about him.

"You're lucky to have someone like her."

"I really am. Thanks." She put the vase on the middle of the wooden kitchen table and sat down. Joe took a seat across from her. He held on to his knees under the table, forcing himself to relax.

"So," she said, as if searching for what to say. "Where do you live again?"

His mind scrambled as he tried to figure out what to say. He didn't have a whole lot of time, and this was his chance to make some progress with her.

"I'm from a small town in Colorado. H-H-H—" He stopped, feeling like an idiot. "Let me try that again," he said with a nervous laugh. This time, instead of saying Havenwood Falls, he went with a town nearby. "I'm from Montrose, Colorado. It's a small town near Telluride. I'm just here visiting."

"Oh," she said, looking confused. "But I thought you said we'd seen each other around."

Joe had forgotten he'd said that at the hospital. He had to think fast.

"Well, I've been here before, so that's what I meant," he said. He hated lying to her and quickly redirected the conversation. "Have you, um, been to Colorado?" he asked, hoping to spark a memory in her.

"Actually, yes. I was there this past Christmas."

"Oh yeah? Where did you go in Colorado? What did you do?" he probed.

"My mom and I went to Breckenridge for the holidays." Her

eyes took on a faraway look, as if she'd been sucked into a sad memory.

"We don't have to talk about it," Joe offered. He started to reach across the table for her hand but stopped himself.

"No, it's okay. Jan said I should never stop talking about my mom or remembering her. She said my stories will keep her alive. And I want to keep her alive. She was my mom and my best friend."

Her sorrow-filled big brown eyes tugged at his heart. And this time, he couldn't stop himself. He reached over, took her hand, and squeezed. She gave him a curious look, making him think the gesture might be too much. He started to let go, when she held on.

"Are you sure we don't know each other? I mean, it may sound crazy, but I swear I know you."

She knew him! She really and truly knew him! But what should he say? He didn't want to scare her or freak her out.

"No, it's not crazy at all." He leaned toward her. "In fact, I feel the same way."

She leaned closer to him, too. "You do?"

"Yes, I do. It's like . . ." He stopped so he could search for the right words.

"We've been together," they said at the same time.

Infiniti's lips parted in surprise. "We just said the same thing."

"We sure did," Joe said, wanting to get closer to her, but the table was in the way.

The front door opened, then slammed shut. Joe pulled his hand away from Infiniti's and sat back as Jan came in with two brown sacks of groceries. He got to his feet right away.

"Here, let me help you."

"Oh, the young man from the hospital. Thank you," Jan said. "Joe, is it?"

"Yes, my name is Joe. And you're welcome." He took the bags and set them on the table. "Are there any other bags?"

"No other bags. Thank you for asking."

Jan spotted the flowers right away. "How thoughtful of you to come by and bring flowers."

Infiniti got to her feet. "Yeah," she said. "Aren't they beautiful?"

"I should say so," Jan replied.

"It was the least I could do." Joe shoved his hands in his jean pockets, not really sure what he should do now that Jan was there.

Jan rubbed her forehead. "I'll leave you two, if that's okay. The hectic evening and the trip to the store has worn me out, and I could use a rest."

Before Joe could respond, Infiniti asked, "Is it okay if Joe stays for a while?"

"Of course. He is more than welcome to stay." Jan patted Joe on the shoulder, then shuffled away, leaving him and Infiniti alone again.

"So," Infiniti said, fiddling with her long, wavy brown hair. "Do you want to go to the other room where it's more comfortable?"

"Sure," Joe said, excited to get closer to her.

He followed Infiniti out of the kitchen and into the living room. They sat on a fluffy oversized white couch. They angled their bodies so they'd be facing each other.

Infiniti leaned her head against the couch cushion. "Tell me about yourself, Joseph Greg."

Something about the way she said Joseph Greg made him want to pounce her. He didn't know if it was her Texas accent, her natural beauty, or a combination of the two, but he forced himself to stay calm. And even though they'd had a similar conversation back home in December, he didn't mind doing it all over again. He could talk to her for hours.

"Well, it's just me, my little brother who's twelve, and my parents. My mom makes jewelry out of the house, and my dad is a police officer."

"A police officer? Wow, what's that like?"

"It actually sucks." He laughed. "My dad knows everything I'm doing before I even do it, so it's hard to get away with stuff."

She smiled. "That does sound sucky."

He shrugged, thinking about how his parents had stepped in to help him with the doc and the Court. "It does, but it's not all bad."

Infiniti interlocked her fingers with his as if it was the most natural thing to do, but then realized what she was doing and dropped his hand.

"I'm, uh, sorry."

"No, don't be sorry," he said, boldly taking her hand back.

This time she didn't let go. Playing with her fingers, he tried to think of a way to ask her about herself without eliciting a fresh wave of sorrow. Luckily for him, she started talking.

"Well, as for me, it's just me and my mom. She's a single mom, so it's always just the two of us." Her voice cracked. "I guess I should say was and not is, since she's not here anymore."

Her eyes watered over. She leaned into him and cried into his chest. He held her gently and rubbed her back. "Everything will be okay, Infiniti."

She pulled back and looked into his eyes. "Will it? Because I feel like it won't."

He wiped the tears from her cheeks, his heart exploding with so much love for her it hurt. He traced her face with his fingertips.

"Of course it will."

Their eyes locked. Their bodies moved closer together.

"Joe," she whispered. "I don't understand it, but I have really strong feelings for you."

"I know what you mean."

"You do?"

"Yes, I most certainly do."

She leaned closer, her eyes closed. Their lips were about to meet when Jan burst into the room. A terrified expression plastered her face. She was clutching her shirt at her chest, taking in frantic breaths.

"My dear!" she called out. "You are in grave danger!"

CHAPTER 10

$\mathcal{F}$leet left Joe and Infiniti and walked across the street. He stared at the damaged and charred structure. From his vantage point, and from what he remembered when he had charged into the flames, the brunt of the fire had blazed to the left of the home and at the rear. Luckily for Infiniti, her room was upstairs on the right. Her mom, on the other hand, had no chance with her room downstairs and in the thick of the flames. Fleet figured the fire must've started in her room.

Focusing on the spot where the ambulance had parked, he walked around, searching for Joe's necklace. Finding nothing, he canvassed the sidewalk and yard.

Still nothing.

He ducked under the yellow caution tape around the house and headed inside. He eyed the space all around the foyer. The stench of water-soaked soot assaulted him as he picked his way over clumps of ash. Keeping a laser focus for any hint of a chain or a stone, he went upstairs and made his way to the first bedroom on the right.

The space exuded Tiny with its purple-on-purple color scheme. The waterlogged room had purple walls, a purple rug, and a giant purple *I* painted on her door. The only break in the color scheme was a soggy white comforter. Dark splotches of carbon marred the walls and ceiling, and a thin layer of ash covered the drenched belongings.

He moved around slowly, eyeing every inch of the floor, but didn't see a necklace. He turned to head back out when a voice spoke to him from behind.

"Leaving so soon, Fleet the Transhuman?"

Fleet froze. His body tingled with icy dread. He recognized the gravelly, deep voice right away. He turned around with slow steps and saw Death in the middle of the room. Tall and wide, dressed in his perfectly tailored black suit, he narrowed his dark menacing eyes on Fleet.

Death kept away from Transhumans for the most part, satisfied to have Tavion taking on the role of the villain, even if Tavion acted independently. Some beings were pure evil without Death's influence.

"What the hell do you want?" Fleet asked.

Death lifted his chin. He huffed. "I could kill you on the spot for being a smart-ass, you know, but I'd prefer to keep you alive. You and your people have provided me much entertainment over the centuries." He clicked his tongue. "Much entertainment."

Fleet clenched his jaw. "Then what is it?"

He knew the monster wanted Tiny, but waited for confirmation.

Death studied Fleet for a long intimidating moment. "It's this human. Infiniti Clausman. She keeps eluding me. Here, in the future, in this reality, in an alternate, she keeps dodging my sentence. Frankly, I'm fucking tired of it. My faithful servant Shade is also weary of her. And so, lucky you, or I should say lucky her, I've decided to handle her demise myself. Once and for all. But not before a little gamesmanship."

Fleet's head reeled. He scrambled for something to say, anything to keep Tiny safe. He thought of offering a trade, but feared Death would want Dominique or even his brother, Farrell. Or maybe even

Joe. He imagined how shitty that would be, Joe trying to save his true love only to trade places with her. Death operated on the cruelest possible level. No way could Fleet risk that. Besides, trading a life for another life was never the solution. He knew that already.

Fleet eyed the window. The sky outside was starting to grow dark. Soon it would have been twenty-four hours for Joe, which meant he only had another forty-eight left. Maybe if he could get Joe and Infiniti safely to Havenwood Falls, the people there could find a way to protect them. He only needed to stall Death long enough for him to accomplish the task.

"How long does she have?" Fleet asked.

Death's lip curled with amused satisfaction. A wide, toothy, ultra-bright grin spread across his angular, clean-shaven face. "Maybe now. Maybe a day. Maybe a week." He shrugged his shoulders. "It's hard to know. But I wanted to alert you of my design. I like seeing you squirm."

Even though Fleet knew none of his attacks would work on the bloodless beast, he wanted nothing more than to charge him head on. But he held back.

Fleet clenched his fists at his side. "Give it your best shot."

He turned his back on Death and started walking out of the room. After a few steps, he heard a swish. He knew Death had left, but he refused to look back. No way in hell would he give that maniac any kind of satisfaction. He needed to play it cool, even if on the inside he was ready to explode.

He scanned the hallway once more for the necklace, then the stairs, and then the foyer before he walked with speed back to the house across the street. He rang the doorbell.

The old woman from the hospital cracked the door open. She peered out. She sighed with relief when she saw Fleet and swung the door open all the way.

"Thank goodness it's you. Come in, hurry."

She ushered him to the living room, where he was surprised to see Joe and Infiniti hand in hand. It seemed whatever he had said to her worked. But then he noticed something else in their expressions.

Fear.

"What happened?" he asked Joe.

"It's Infiniti. Death is after her."

Fleet's blood boiled with anger. The menacing beast was wasting no time with his mission. "How do you know?"

"He told me," Jan said with a worried frown. "I was taking a nap, and he spoke to me through my dreams." She glanced up and away as if going back to that moment. "I dreamed I was in the kitchen, cutting vegetables for soup. A gust of wind blew over me, and a swishing sound filled the room. When I turned to see what it was, I saw a thick man sitting at my kitchen table. He wore a black suit and had dark penetrating eyes. The kind of eyes that look endless. He spoke to me in a deep, throaty voice. He told me his name was Death, and that he was coming for Infiniti. He disappeared, and then I woke up."

Jan wrapped her arms around herself, as if the recollection of her conversation with Death chilled her to the bone.

Infiniti put her hand on Jan's arm. "He sent me a message too," she said to Fleet. "When I was leaving the hospital, I saw a note by the elevator from Death saying he was coming for me. I thought I was seeing things, so I ignored it. But now I know I wasn't imaging anything after all." Infiniti lowered her voice. "He's coming for me."

Fleet ran his fingers through his dark hair. "He came to me too, just now when I was across the street. He's probably the one that started the fire at your house."

Nobody spoke for a few minutes as everything sank in. Fleet eyed Infiniti and Jan, thinking they were taking everything in stride.

"You two seem oddly okay with all this."

"Okay with Death being a terrorizing entity after Infiniti? And responsible for killing her mother?" Jan asked. "Not in the least! He is a vile despicable being! But do I believe it's all real?" She sighed. "Sadly, I do. I also believe Infiniti saw a reaper. I'm a psychic, so I understand a thing or two about the unexplained."

Fleet shot Joe a look. "Joe, she understands the unexplained. Probably Infiniti too. I'd say now would be a good time to get everything out in the open."

Infiniti eyed Joe. "Get what out in the open?"

Fleet hung back and let Joe take over. The lovestruck guy rubbed the back of his neck. He faced Infiniti as if she were the only person in the room.

"Well," Joe said, pausing to formulate his next words. "What I'm about to say may sound crazy, but please hear me out. And please believe me. Okay?"

Infiniti nodded with wide eyes. "Okay."

Joe blew out a breath. He shoved his hands in his pockets. "The thing is, I'm from the future. Six years into the future, to be exact. We met when you went to Breckenridge this past Christmas, but you didn't exactly make it to Breckenridge. Your car crashed and you ended up in my town. You just don't remember any of it."

Infiniti sucked in her breath. She held it for a time before saying, "I always dream of car crashes. Mostly they happen in the snow, with me driving off a cliff. Are you saying that really happened? I mean, I would've remembered something like that. Right?"

"Yes, it really happened." Joe let that soak in before he continued. "After your crash in December 2012, you were taken by ambulance to my town. Once there, you and Fleet ended up time traveling to December 2018 because you needed a spell to protect you from evil magic. You don't remember any of your time there because your memories of the town were wiped when you left my time and came back to your own. Both yours and Fleet's. But while you were there in my time, we met, and we spent a lot of time together, and we . . ."

"Fell in love," she whispered.

"Yes," he said. "We did." He waited a few seconds before he

went on. "When you left, you told me to find you, and I said I would. And while I searched for a way to get to you, I started feeling like you were in danger."

"The fire," she whispered.

"Yes, the fire," Joe said.

Infiniti turned to face Fleet. "You don't remember any of this either?"

"Not a thing. But I've done enough and seen enough to believe it."

Even though Infiniti looked shell-shocked, Fleet thought it best for Joe to get everything out. "But there's more," Fleet prompted. "Right, Joe?"

Infiniti placed her hand up by her throat. "There's more?"

"Dear spirits," Jan whispered. "There's more than the reaper, the fire, the messages from Death, the car crash Infiniti doesn't remember, and the time travel?"

Joe cleared his throat. He wiped his hands on his jeans. "There's nothing worse than that, but I haven't explained why I'm here yet."

"Oh," Infiniti muttered. "That's right, you haven't."

Joe moved closer to Infiniti. "When you left, I became lovesick. As in, really, really sick, because my love for you is a forever thing."

Her brows stitched together. "A forever thing?"

"Yes, a forever thing. You see, I'm a"—he paused for a really long second—"a wolf shifter."

Infiniti's mouth fell open. She didn't say anything, so he went on.

"My feelings for you were so deep and so intense that I was called to you, and I will remain called to you forever."

Joe stopped again so Infiniti could take it all in. Fleet watched, waiting for her to say something.

"You're . . . a . . . wolf shifter," she repeated.

"Yes," Joe answered. "I am."

"Are you here to ask Infiniti to go back with you to your time?" Jan asked, connecting the dots.

"Yes," Joe said. "To my town and my time, 2019."

"Oh," Infiniti said, taking on an expression of understanding. "Six years into the future," she whispered. "To Montrose, Colorado."

Joe pointed at Fleet, signaling him to correct her. "To Havenwood Falls, Colorado," Fleet clarified. "Joe's spelled so that he can't say the name of the town or talk about it too much."

"Then why can you say it?" Infiniti asked.

"It's a long story," Fleet said, not feeling like getting into how he knew about the town. Besides, it was totally irrelevant where she was concerned.

"Oh," she said.

Joe moved in front of Infiniti, as if nobody else was in the room. "As soul mates, we're linked. And we belong together. That is, if you feel the same way and want to come with me."

Infiniti sank down to the couch while a look of bewilderment spread across her face. Joe knelt on the floor in front of her. He took her hands.

"It's a lot, I know."

Fleet crossed his arms. Death's smug expression replayed in his mind. He needed to impress upon Infiniti the gravity of the situation.

"Listen, Tiny. Joe's right. It is a lot. But we don't have the luxury of time to go over everything in more detail. Death is coming. Getting you to Havenwood Falls may be your only chance for survival."

CHAPTER 11

*I*nfiniti couldn't believe what she was hearing, but at the same time, also could believe it. The feeling of missing something or someone had been growing in her since the Cold Moon. Add the dreams of car crashes and the visit from Abigail, and it all made sense.

She'd been missing Joe.

Gazing into his hazel eyes as he knelt before her, she could feel the intense connection with him. But to learn he was a wolf shifter from a town of supernaturals and that she needed to go with him to the future because Death wanted to kill her? It was a lot to take in.

Death had taken her mom and now he wanted her. She knew her mom would say to fight like hell and do whatever she could to be safe. But leave her home? And go to the future with Joe? She wasn't sure.

Infiniti looked to Jan, the closest person to her alive. She trusted Jan and knew Jan had her best interests at heart.

"What should I do?"

Jan pursed her lips, then gave a swift nod. "You live."

Live? She already had to live without her mom, but what about everything else? But then she remembered she didn't really have anything else. Her house was gone. She didn't have any other family. Her friends had all left for college. Trent had said he'd come see her, but he'd be a few days.

"And if living means leaving you and everything I've ever known? And going to a town six years in the future?" she asked Jan.

"Then you leave here and go to a town six years in the future. And I'll come visit you, in six years. With more wrinkles and more gray hair."

Infiniti eyed Joe. "Can she do that? Come visit me?"

"Of course," he said, releasing her hands and sitting next to her. "The supernatural power of the town doesn't prevent us from having visitors. And unless someone is a supe, no one even knows about the magic." He lifted his shoulders. "It's really just a normal and beautiful place. You can work, go to school, all of it. You can even come visit Jan, without the time travel part that is. You'll just have to follow the magical rules of the town. I can fill you in on all that when you get there. If you decide to come with me, that is."

Infiniti thought about seeing Jan in six years and how weird that would be. And then she wondered if Jan would even be alive in six years. She pushed those morbid thoughts away, telling herself Jan had way more than six years left in her.

"And you'll be well taken care of," Jan added. "Your mother had a two-million-dollar insurance policy with you as the beneficiary."

Infiniti gulped. "She did?" Tears sprang to her eyes. It was just like her mom to do that. She was always doing whatever she could for Infiniti. And that's when Infiniti knew she needed to do whatever she could for her mom.

And that included living.

She brought her attention to Joe, the wolf shifter she had met in the future and fallen in love with, who had come to the past to save her. Her heart and soul hadn't forgotten him, even though her mind had.

"I'd like to talk to Joe alone for a minute," she said to Jan and Fleet.

"Sure," Fleet nodded.

"We'll be in the other room," Jan added.

Infiniti folded and unfolded her hands in her lap while she processed everything. Joe placed his hands on top of hers, his touch instantly calming her. She stared at their intertwined hands.

"Yesterday I was cleaning my room, trying to make sense of my future. Today my whole world has changed."

"I know," Joe said. "And I'm so sorry. Your life may never be the same, but I promise it can still be amazing."

"If we can make it out of here," she tacked on.

"We'll make it," Joe urged, his eyes taking on a fiery look. "I know it."

Seeing the determination in him ignited the spirit of her old self that had been buried under her grief. Her mom didn't raise a quitter. She decided to hold on to who she was, no matter how hard. She wasn't going to let Death win. With Joe and Fleet on her side, and with Jan's support, she felt like everything would turn out okay.

"All right," she said, deciding to take a huge leap of faith. "I'll go with you."

A look of surprise mixed with relief washed over Joe. "You will?"

She smiled. "Yes, I will."

His gaze drifted to her lips, lingering there for a quick second before coming back up to her eyes. The vulnerability of the move made her heart flutter and her insides tremble. He was the perfect blend of sexy and adorable, and in that moment she wanted nothing more than to feel his lips on hers. He must've felt the same way, because he scooted closer.

"It's terrible timing, Infiniti, but I really need to kiss you."

"I need to kiss you, too," she said, giving in to her impulses.

They moved closer and closer to each other. Their mouths opened, their lips met, and finally they kissed. It was sweet and tender and familiar and provocative. Her head soared in the clouds while longing spread throughout her body.

She parted from him slowly, not wanting to break away, but feeling weird that Jan and Fleet were in the other room.

"Wow," Joe said.

"Very wow," she echoed.

Unable to stop themselves, they kissed again. This time they swooped in and wrapped their arms around each other. It was the kind of embrace that came from being scared of losing something new and wonderful. And if she could, she'd stay like that with him forever. But they didn't have forever. She figured they needed to tell the others about her decision. Especially since time wasn't on their side.

"I guess we should call Jan and Fleet back in," she said against his lips between panting breaths.

"Probably."

He kissed her once more before they separated completely. He got off the couch and helped her to feet.

"Jan, Fleet," she called out, smoothing her long brown hair away from her face. "Y'all can come back now."

Together again in the living room, Infiniti announced, "I've decided to go."

"That's my girl," Jan said.

Fleet rubbed his hands together. "With that settled, I suggest we get a move on."

"You mean leave now?" Terror struck Infiniti, along with the realization that all she had was the clothes on her back, clothes that Jan had purchased for her while she was in the hospital. Jeans, a plain white T-shirt, and white tennis shoes. "What I'm wearing is all I have. Everything else is ruined."

Jan placed her hands on Infiniti's shoulders. "I'm sure they have nice stores where you're going. And if they don't, you raise a fuss."

Infiniti hugged Jan tightly. "I will."

"Good," Jan said, ending their embrace with a reassuring rub on the back. She motioned to Fleet. "This young man will come back here after he's seen you and Joe safely to Havenwood Falls, and he'll help me get your money to you." She smiled. "And then I'll see you in six years. Easy peasy."

Infiniti nodded and smiled while her stomach clenched. There was that phrase, the one Jan always used for things that were anything but easy. She mustered up her courage and swallowed the lump in her throat.

"Easy peasy," she repeated back.

Tinker trotted into the room. She rubbed her furry body against Infiniti's legs, purring loudly. Infiniti crouched down to pet her, still marveling at how she wasn't all white anymore but now understanding why. When she stood back up, Trent popped into her mind. He said he'd be coming to see her. She wondered if she should call him, but quickly decided against it, because what would she say?

"Jan, Trent's supposed to be coming to see me."

"I'll handle it all, dear. Don't you worry."

Forcing herself to keep a stiff upper lip, she nodded. Hand in hand with Joe, she went outside with him and Fleet to their car. Before she got in, she stopped and studied her house across the street. Memories of good times flashed before her eyes—movie nights with friends, parties, conversations with her mom. She vowed to keep the memories and love alive inside her. She also vowed to somehow return to Houston again. And then she started imagining what Jan would say to explain her disappearance. She hoped it wasn't something completely off the rails, like joining the circus or a monastery. As if any of her friends would believe a monastery cover story. The circus, maybe.

Fleet drove while Infiniti sat in the back with Joe. Fleet suspected he'd have better luck transporting her and Joe six years into the future to Havenwood Falls if he could get as close to the town as possible. But since Fleet didn't know exactly where the town was, and Joe couldn't say because of the protective magic that bound him, they settled on getting to Montrose, the nearest city Joe could talk about.

Minutes turned into hours, day turned into night, and a sense of safety started to set in. Maybe Death would let them go. Maybe he was busy with other things. With her mind a little at ease, Infiniti turned her attention to Joe. She wanted to know all about him and their time together. How did they meet? Where did she stay? What did they do?

She scooted closer to Joe as he filled her in on everything she didn't remember. Staring into his dreamy hazel eyes and admiring his perfectly angular features, she listened to their love story. As he spoke, everything about him drew her in—his smile, his laugh, the way he traced her hand with his fingers but slowly pulled them away because he didn't know if it was too much, but then went back to touching her again because he couldn't help himself. She didn't want him to stop. She might have had her doubts when he first told her everything, but being with him made her heart swell and the entire world around them melt away. It was just her, Joe, and the amazing connection between them she had felt right away but didn't understand.

After a while, she realized how exhausted she was. But before she could sleep, she needed to go to the bathroom.

"Hey, Fleet, I really need to make a stop."

"Okay," he said. "I saw a sign for a rest stop a couple of miles ahead."

The hot August night sky was sprinkled with a host of shimmery stars, stars Infiniti really couldn't see from home because Houston was so bright and big. Finally she spotted a neon blinking sign that promised *Tasty Jerky* and *Clean Restrooms*.

Fleet parked in a spot farthest away from the entrance. He turned off the car. He thrummed his thumbs against the steering wheel. "We go in fast and get out fast. Everyone stay close. Got it?"

A wave of shivers raced across Infiniti's spine. The fear and panic that had disappeared sprang fresh inside of her. She eyed the busy parking lot and watched people either pumping gas in their cars or filtering in and out of the store.

"We'll be okay with all the activity, right?" She let out a nervous laugh. "You know, safety in numbers and all that?"

"Should be," Fleet said.

"I'll be right beside you," Joe reassured her.

"Me too, Tiny." Fleet eyed her through the rearview mirror. "Now let's do this."

Infiniti laced her fingers with Joe's and held him close to her as they followed Fleet into the busy store. They hurried to the back, where the restrooms were. Infiniti paused as she stared at the separate section for women.

She gulped, eyeing Joe. "I have to go alone," she said, not wanting to leave him, suddenly wishing she had squatted behind the car instead. But they were already inside. It was too late to go back now.

"I'll be right here," Joe promised. "It'll be fine."

Slowly releasing her hold from his, she went in. She made her way to the first empty stall and did her business fast. When she came out, she went to the sink and started lathering her hands. Glancing at herself in the mirror, she saw thick red letters sprawled across the glass.

YOUR TIME IS COMING

Infiniti shrieked, and Joe bolted into the restroom.

"What is it?" He glanced about. "What happened?"

She pointed at the glass. Her hand shook like uncontrollably. "There was a m-m-message, right there. But now it's g-g-gone."

Fleet ran in, followed by a stout female worker wearing jeans and a company logo shirt.

"Everything okay?" she asked with a Texas twang. "I heard screaming."

"Uh, she fell," Joe hurried out. "And she yelled. But she's fine now. Everything is okay now."

Infiniti stilled her hands by shoving them in her jeans pockets. "Yeah, I slipped. But I'm okay."

The woman nodded, while studying the floor as if looking for a slippery spot.

Fleet jerked his chin to the exit. "We'll get out of your way, ma'am."

They filed out of the restroom and left the store in a hurry. Infiniti's heart raced out of control. Her nerves were on edge and her eyes flickered about as she wondered if Death would deliver another message.

Fleet sped out of the parking lot, increasing their distance from the store. He slowed down enough to join the flow of traffic. Maintaining a steady speed, he said, "Let's hear it, Tiny. What did the message say?"

Infiniti had been working on her breathing to steady herself. "It said, 'Your time is coming.'"

"Not if I can help it," Joe said.

Infiniti stayed on the edge of her seat. She eyed their surroundings, as if Death would fall down on them from above, when she noticed the weather changing. The dim streetlights that dotted the sides of the roads illuminated with enough light for them to see thick puffs of clouds gathering overhead. The mass stretched out as far as the eye could see. Pellets of rain started hammering the car. The winds gusted so hard the car rocked from side to side.

"This is tornado weather," Infiniti warned, scooting closer to Joe. She searched the horizon, looking for a break in the clouds, but didn't see one. "Is Death doing this?"

"Probably," Fleet said. He kept both hands on the steering wheel, holding it in a firm grip. His jaw clenched. "But don't worry, I got this."

Infiniti and Joe sat back. They stayed close together. "You know what would really suck?" she asked him.

"You mean, what would suck more than this weather and Death being after us?" He smiled, trying to lighten a terrifying situation.

She wanted to laugh too, but suddenly couldn't. Her heart had been through too much. "What would suck is reuniting with you only for both of us to die. Then I'd be losing two loved ones."

He traced the side of her face with his fingers and tucked her hair behind her ear. "Yeah," he whispered. "That would really suck. Luckily for us, that's not gonna happen."

The storm clouds and the hard rain followed them as they made their way from Texas to New Mexico. On edge, making quick stops, trading off naps with Joe, it was the worst and most stressful road trip of her life. Yet each mile they advanced and each city they passed, hope that they'd make it grew inside of her.

Maybe Death had found someone else to torment.

They arrived in Colorado well into the next day. Driving into the plains with majestic mountains off in the distance, Infiniti noticed the sky clearing a little. The ominous dark clouds were giving way to slivers of blue sky.

"I think we've made it through the storm," Infiniti said with reserved optimism. She kept peering about, looking for the sun, but didn't see it. "At least, I think we have."

"I think you're right," Joe said, craning his neck and looking out the window too. "I think the worst is behind us now."

"Maybe," Fleet said. He glanced over his shoulder at Joe. "A few more hours and we'll be in Montrose. And then this will all be over."

Infiniti sat back in her seat. Something in Fleet's tone and choice of words told her he didn't share the same outlook as Joe. And whatever he was feeling filtered into her. Her stomach twisted into a brand new knot. Any sense of hope she'd been storing up started slipping away.

Joe placed his hand on her knee. "We're gonna make it," he whispered.

Infiniti thought of losing her mother. She never wanted to feel that level of pain ever again. And then she remembered asking Jan what she should do, and Jan telling her to live. She resolved to do exactly that. For herself, for her mother, for Jan, and even for Joe, who had crossed six years of time to find her. She was going to push every shred of fear and doubt out of her mind and fight for her survival.

After a quick snooze and a few more hours of driving, Fleet turned onto a small two-lane dirt road hidden between massive pine trees. He slowed down as the car worked its way over bumps and rocks. After a while, they came upon a clearing and parked on the far side of the open space. Everyone got out of the car quietly, as if Death hovered nearby, watching and listening.

Fleet rubbed his hands together. He intertwined his fingers and popped his knuckles. "This is it. You both ready?"

"Yeah," Infiniti and Joe said at the same time.

"Good," Fleet said. "Now let's stand in a circle and hold hands. Joe, you concentrate hard on where you want to go."

Fleet walked to the middle of the clearing. Infiniti and Joe followed. They started getting into position when a deep, menacing laughter filled the air.

"Look at the three of you, joining hands in a kumbaya moment. How pathetic."

An army of goosebumps raced across Infiniti's skin when she saw Death. Or, at least, she thought it was Death. She'd never seen him before. He was a towering figure, dressed in an all-black suit. He was leaning against the car with his arms folded.

"You're dead. I mean, Death," she muttered.

His thin lips curled into a menacing smile. "I am indeed. To both. And you're about to join me. I hope you're ready." He licked his lips. "I know I am."

CHAPTER 12

*J*oe eyed the dark, hulking figure standing by the car. He halfway expected a skeletal figure in a grim reaper outfit, but instead Death was dressed in all black, like the owner of a funeral home. And he may as well have been one. He took souls for a living.

Joe glanced at Infiniti. Dark circles encased her terror-filled eyes. Her skin had paled from her grief. He needed her to hold on a little longer despite Death's threats.

She's not going anywhere with you," he said, sidling in front of Infiniti.

"Of course she is," Death sneered. He eased himself from his resting position beside the car and brushed off his suit jacket. He approached with slow, calculated steps.

Fleet moved beside Joe. His hands crackled with energy.

"You and Infiniti run when I say," he urged in a low whisper.

Letting them know he could hear them, Death taunted, "Run? Please do. I welcome a good ol' fashioned game of chase. We can even play tag. I'll be it, of course."

Death moved closer. His sparkling toothy grin covered half his face. He lifted his hand and swiped the air with his fingers. A snapping sound filled the space all around them, followed by a crackling of splintering wood as a massive tree came crashing down. Fleet flung out a stream of energy, blasting the timbering pine into smithereens. Leaves and branches showered all around them.

"I am having so much fun with the three of you," Death chided, still smiling, still advancing. "It'll be a shame when all this is over. But when your time is up, it's up."

Joe scanned the area, looking for a place to run and hide with Infiniti. He started backing up with her when Fleet powered up his energy. He hurled a series of blasts at Death that were easily deflected by the towering monster, as if he were batting away at bubbles.

"Shit," Fleet muttered.

"One of yours for one of mine," Death countered.

Death frowned. He narrowed his eyes. He raised his hands and clawed at the air with angry force. Explosive blasts erupted all around. Trees and shrubs careened through the air. Fleet flung his energy streams, deflecting the onslaught while Joe knocked Infiniti to the ground and covered her with his body. She buried her face in the crook of his neck and held onto him for dear life as the ground beneath them shook like an earthquake.

And then, all at once, the melee stopped.

Infiniti hugged Joe while her body trembled. "Is it over?"

Joe lifted his head. He peered about. The place looked like a tornado had barreled through the clearing. Clumps of trees and debris covered the ground as far as the eye could see. Joe caught a glimpse of Fleet leaning over in the middle of the disaster, hands on his knees, but otherwise looking okay. He didn't see Death anywhere.

"I don't think so," Joe answered. As a wolf shifter, he knew hunters never released their prey. And Death was the ultimate hunter. He got up and helped Infiniti to her feet. He spun around, searching the area for the madman as he approached Fleet, but he didn't see him. He placed his hand on Fleet's shoulder.

"Fleet, you okay?"

Fleet rose to a standing position. "That son of bitch is playing with us," he said, gulping for air. "Do you see him?"

Joe pulled Infiniti close. He kept scanning the field, his wolf shifter eyes and ears kicking into high gear.

"No, I don't."

"Should we hurry and do the transport now? Before he comes back?" Infiniti asked in a panic-filled tone.

A cackling laugh whispered through the winds. A flock of crows started gathering overhead, cawing as they began flying in a circle formation.

"Son of a bitch," Fleet said under his breath.

"What now?" Joe asked.

"Now I call for backup," Fleet answered. "Hold on."

Joe watched Fleet close his eyes. His lips moved as he mumbled under his breath. When he opened his eyes, a flash of lightning crashed all around him. When the light faded, a guy who looked just like Fleet but with blond hair appeared. He marched over to Fleet's side. Joe thought for sure they were brothers.

"What's happening?" the guy asked Fleet, acknowledging Joe and Infiniti with a quick nod.

"These two need to get to Havenwood Falls, but Death is being an asshole."

"Okay, and the plan?"

"Put a protective shield around us while I get them home."

"Okay," the guy said. "Let's go."

Fleet eyed Joe and Infiniti. "Get together," he commanded, moving toward them. "And hold hands."

Joe moved even closer to Infiniti. He grabbed her hands as the crows cried louder, their swarm flying closer. The newcomer knelt down in front of Joe and Infiniti. He placed his hands on the ground. Streams of white mist poured out of his arms and hands, oozing underneath their feet and then stretching upward, forming into a vaporized bubble that grew until it encased their group like a shimmering dome.

"Whoa," Infiniti whispered.

"Okay, Fleet," the guy said between clenched lips. "Do it."

Fleet placed one hand on Infiniti's wrist and the other on Joe's. "Think of your time and your place," Fleet ordered Joe.

Joe nodded, keeping his eyes on the skies as the black birds started dive bombing them, sizzling away as they made contact with the supernatural shield. He forced himself to keep calm as the birds gathered in so tightly, their chaotic movement blocked out everything else.

"Oh my god," Infiniti muttered, flinching at each black-winged strike against the energy surrounding them.

"It's gonna be okay," Joe urged. "Just focus on me."

"Joe! Think of where you want to go!" Fleet hollered.

Focusing on his directive, he embraced Infiniti in a bear hug. He lowered his eyes. He thought of Havenwood Falls and his family, but his concentration kept breaking with the clamoring and commotion all around him.

"My home," he said out loud, thinking the verbal command would help him stay focused. Repeating his destination, he caught sight of Fleet's gray power. It seeped out all over the place until the ground started churning with power.

"My home," Joe repeated, struggling to block out everything else when he noticed a group of birds landing on the barrier. Joe watched in horror as they hammered at the sphere with their beaks like possessed demons, despite the zapping that shocked them with each peck. One made it through the enclosure, and then another. They bounced all around like crazed pinballs inside Fleet's contained energy storm.

"Hurry," the guy urged Fleet. "I can't hold it much longer."

"Just a little more," Fleet grunted out.

Joe squeezed Infiniti even tighter to him, thinking of his home, trying desperately to keep the image in his mind, when a feeling of weightlessness swept over him. A supersonic boom shook him to his core as he felt Fleet release his hold, and he and Infiniti plunged into a free fall.

CHAPTER 13

*J*oe held on to Infiniti as they toppled to the ground amidst an explosion of dirt and electric particles. He cradled Infiniti's head, waiting for everything to stop, then cautiously scanned the area. The birds were gone. The leveled field was gone, too, replaced with tall grass and mid-sized trees.

"Did we make it?" Infiniti asked, uncovering her face.

From the look of the growth all around them, they had definitely time traveled. He had to assume he was in the same spot but in his proper time.

"I think so," Joe answered, getting up and helping her to her feet.

Infiniti smiled. "I think so, too."

There was no shield. The blond-haired guy that Joe assumed was Fleet's brother, because they looked so much alike, was gone too. Only Fleet remained, standing nearby. Death had to have been left behind.

"Hey, Fleet, did we make it?"

Fleet dusted off his pants. He turned and smiled, and Joe staggered back. Fleet's eyes had turned from green to pure black. Infiniti clutched Joe's arm in a death grip.

"Oh no," she uttered.

Joe pushed Infiniti behind him and stepped back, increasing the distance between them and Fleet.

"What have you done with Fleet?" Joe demanded.

Death formed a ball of electricity in Fleet's hands. He tossed it in the air and caught it with his other hand.

"Nothing," he said in Fleet's voice. "I'm merely trying him on for size. I have always been a huge fan of Transhumans. Really, any humans."

Death smiled, then morphed from Fleet's form into Infiniti's mom. Like Infiniti, she was petite with long wavy hair, but instead of rich brown locks, her hair was strewn with white streaks.

"Infiniti," Death said in a hoarse voice. Her face started crisping with burn marks. "Why did you leave my cold, dead body in Houston? What kind of daughter are you? Don't you love me? Or was that all a lie?"

Infiniti gasped, digging her nails into Joe's skin. "You monster," she choked out between anger-filled tears.

Joe turned Infiniti away. "Ignore him."

Death let out a booming laugh. His form blurred and stretched as it changed from Infiniti's mom to Joe's dad.

"Son, you've always been such a huge disappointment to me." Death crossed his arms and shook his head, sounding exactly like his dad, complete with the same mannerisms. "A huge disappointment."

Rage coursed through Joe's veins. Everything he had felt since the Cold Moon Ball mounted inside of him—heartache, pain, and fury—until everything boiled over and erupted inside of him.

"Back away," he ordered Infiniti.

His bones started cracking. His teeth elongated. His nails transformed into claws. He grunted as his muscles expanded, then contracted, as his clothes tore away and fur erupted over his skin. He fell over to the ground in wolf form.

Baring his fangs, Joe crouched low to the ground. He growled at Death, who had morphed back to his black-suited form.

"You gonna come at me, wolfy?" Death prodded. "You think you can take me?"

Joe snapped. He crouched low, and then pounced. He swiped at Death's face, then went for the jugular, not even knowing if Death had one, but doing whatever he could to shred the madman who wanted Infiniti.

Blasts of pain zapped Joe. He continued lashing out and biting, despite the agony coursing through his body, until a force slammed into him like an invisible freight train. He sailed through the air and thudded to the ground on his side.

Death marched over to him. He held his hand out, as if ready to choke the life out of him, when Infiniti lunged between them. She covered Joe with her arms, shielding his body.

"Stop! You can have me!" she yelled.

Death halted. He lowered his hand. He looked down on Infiniti as she protected Joe.

"What did you say?" he asked slowly, as if unsure of what he heard.

"Leave him alone and you can have me."

Joe whimpered. He didn't want Infiniti to give herself up for him, but he couldn't move. It felt as if every bone in his body had been pulverized.

Infiniti buried her face in his fur. She kissed his cheek and then stroked his head. "I'm so sorry," she whispered.

She climbed up to her feet. She straightened her spine and raised her chin. "Leave him alone and I'll go with you."

Death narrowed his eyes. He tilted his head. "You will trade your life for this wolf shifter?"

"Yes, I would. And I do. He loves me. And I love him. But you wouldn't know anything about that, would you? Death doesn't love anyone or anything!"

Death considered her words. He did know a thing or two about love. He turned away from the petite human, suddenly overwhelmed with thoughts of his own love. She was the most glorious and beautiful creature, created more than one hundred years ago, and lived in the Japanese underworld. Would she ever know that he loved her? Would she ever return the sentiment? Would she ever sacrifice herself for him?

Infiniti moved in front of Death. She narrowed her eyes while a look of recognition dawned on her face. "You do know. You do love someone."

Death scowled. He raised his hand to swipe at her with his power when she raised her arms.

"You need to tell her. Before it's too late. Before something happens to her and she's taken from you—the way you're going to take me from Joe."

Joe listened intently to Death and Infiniti, and when Infiniti compared herself to the person Death loved, he saw Death's expression shift. Was it doubt? A change of heart? Joe didn't know, but he lifted his head, pointed his muzzle to the sky, and let out a long, agonizing howl. The wail pierced through the cloudy day, drifting with the summer wind, letting every nearby creature know he was about to lose his one true love.

Joe's head fell down in defeat, his heart shattering for Infiniti, when a chorus of howls sounded in the distance. His pain had been heard, and if he and Infiniti had transported to the correct time and place, his pack would be on the move.

Infiniti's arms shook uncontrollably. "I'm just like her," she whispered. "And you're just like Joe."

Death moved closer to her. He glanced at Joe from the corner of his eye.

"Yes, I know something about love. I know the pain of not having it. The cruelty of it not being returned. I know every negative emotion associated with it." He stepped away from Infiniti. "But I've never experienced its joy. Or its pleasure. I don't know any of those things." Death clasped his hands behind his back. "I will let you have these things, human. And maybe one day I'll have the same returned to me. Consider it a quid pro quo. So, for now, you are off the top of my list." He brought his face close to Infiniti's with a swish. Infiniti saw the skeletal features beneath the thin layer of skin and shuddered. "But you are still on the list. And I'll be watching you."

With a gust of wind and a blast of light, Death vanished.

Infiniti lowered her arms. She sank to her knees. She huddled with Joe, holding him to her.

"Please be okay," she whispered. "Please."

Joe could feel the wetness from her tears on his fur. He nuzzled into her, relieved for her to be alive. But now he was broken, literally.

The pounding of animal paws and breaking of twigs rumbled in the distance, moving closer with steady rhythm. As the din grew louder, the earth started shaking.

"Please tell me that sound is your friends," Infiniti said.

A pack of wolves mixed with mountain lions burst onto the scene. The animals paced around Joe and Infiniti, circling them in a protective manner. Infiniti noticed two of the wolves had the same white fur as Joe but looked bigger and older. They stood closest to Joe. Infiniti figured they were his parents.

"It was Death," she said to them. "He did this, but now he's gone."

Suddenly, a tall elfish-looking man appeared out of thin air. He had long ears and a long flat nose. He eyed Joe with concern. "Move aside, young lady," he huffed.

Infiniti did as he said, backing away from Joe. The two white wolves joined her side. She watched as the man placed his hands on Joe. He moved them up and down his fur, holding them longer in some places and shorter in others. He worked methodically, probing and touching until Joe clamored to his paws.

"Joe," the man instructed, "escort this young maiden to the main road. The rest of you," he waved to the animals, "get back home at once."

The man vanished. The mountain lions trotted off, followed by the wolves, with the two white-furred ones lingering a little longer before they took off too. And Joe stayed. He pressed his body against Infiniti's leg and nudged her forward.

She kept her hand on his back. "You almost died, and then the supernatural dream team arrived," she said in an astonished voice. "And that elf guy healed you. And then he disappeared."

Joe huffed.

"Is that what your town is like? I mean, do elves walk around like it's no big deal and people transform into animals like it's nothing?"

He huffed again, wanting to explain everything, but figured it was best for him to still be in wolf form so she could process. They could talk later.

"I'm definitely not in Kansas anymore," she muttered.

They emerged onto a small dirt road. A Jeep was parked on the side. Joe's dad got out of the car and hurried over to them. He got down on his knees in front of Joe and hugged his neck.

"Son, thank God you're okay." He stayed like that for a while before standing up and hugging Infiniti. "And Infiniti, you made it, too. I'm so glad."

"Thank you," she said. "You must be Joe's dad."

"I am," he said. "You can call me Ivan."

He opened the car door and took out a stack of clothes. He placed them on the back bumper. "Infiniti, why don't you get in the car. I'll stay back here with Joe while he changes."

She sat in the back seat. After a few minutes, Joe climbed in next to her. She wrapped her arms around him. "Oh, Joe."

He hugged her back. "We made it," he exhaled. "We really and truly made it."

He wanted to say something about what she had said to Death about her feelings for him, but decided to wait. He wanted to hurry and get to the safety of Havenwood Falls before Death changed his mind about letting Infiniti live. But then he wondered if she still even wanted to go with him now that Death had backed down. He supposed if she wanted to go back to her place and time, the Court would help her.

"Now what?" Infiniti asked.

Joe moved closer to Infiniti. "Now we go to Havenwood Falls, if you still want to come with me."

Infiniti touched her fingers to her lips. She gazed up at Joe. Her expression told him she was thinking about what she should do. She sat quiet for a long time.

"Joe," she finally said. "I haven't felt right since the Cold Moon. But ever since I've been with you, I feel complete. Like with you I'm whole again. Myself again. And I'm not missing anything."

Joe's heart soared. "So you'll come with me?"

She smiled. "Yes."

"With that settled," Joe said, "let's go home."

Joe's dad opened the driver's side door. "Everyone ready?"

"Yeah," Joe said. "We're ready."

He clasped hands with Infiniti. They leaned against each other and sat in silence as they drove home, a deep understanding passing through them over everything they'd been through in such a short amount of time.

They rolled into town, the graying sky turning to night. Joe eyed the streets, realizing they weren't heading home.

"Dad, where are we going?"

"To City Hall. Addie wants to meet you both there."

When they got to the building, all the lights were turned off, and the parking lot was empty. Joe's dad parked at the far end of the lot, and another Jeep pulled up next to them. Addie got out of the other vehicle, and Joe, Infiniti, and Joe's dad exited theirs. Addie lowered her glasses. She studied Joe and then Infiniti.

"I'm impressed," Addie said with a wide smile. "I know rules were broken. We'll talk about all that later and do our big welcome orientation tomorrow, but for now I've got orders to shuttle the both of you to Dr. Underwood for a look over." She pointed at Joe. "Then you will go home." She pointed at Infiniti. "And you will go to my mom Lyra's house. But where are my manners?" Addie stuck her hand out to Infiniti. "You don't remember me yet, but I'm Addie. Addie Beaumont."

"That's right," Infiniti said. "Joe told me my memories from my time here will come back."

"Yep," Addie said. "Everything that happened when you were here will come back. Though I'm not sure when. Could be soon, could take a while since you're a time traveler and all that. It all depends. Now let's go. It's getting late."

After a quick visit with Dr. Underwood, Joe got the all-clear, while Infiniti was told to come back on a regular basis so she could be monitored for any residual side effects of time travel.

"What does that even mean?" Joe asked, as they stood outside waiting for Lyra Beaumont to pick up Infiniti, wondering if he should be worried.

"Apparently I've done so much time hopping, I need to be monitored for a complicated word Dr. Underwood told me that I forgot. He compared it to jet lag on steroids."

"Oh," Joe said. "That doesn't sound so bad."

"No, it doesn't." A hush fell down on them. "So I stayed at this lady's house the last time I was here?"

"Yes, you did. It's a great house with lots of room. And you'll love Ms. Beaumont. She's really cool."

"Oh," she said, suddenly looking unsure of everything.

"I can come over later tonight, or in the morning. Or both. Whatever you want," Joe offered, wanting her to feel comfortable but not wanting to overdo it.

"Tonight would be great. Thanks, Joe."

A car drove up, and Lyra Beaumont got out. She walked over to Joe and Infiniti wearing a huge smile.

"Joseph and Infiniti, reunited. It's so good to see." She hugged Joe and then Infiniti, but caught on right away that Infiniti still didn't remember anything. She stepped back. "My name is Lyra Beaumont, and I'll be your host, Infiniti. Are you ready to go?"

"Yeah, I guess." She turned to Joe. "See you later?"

"Yes, later. I'll be there."

Joe watched as Infiniti walked to the car, looking hesitant and a little scared. She got in the passenger side, and they started to drive off, when the car stopped. The door opened. Infiniti popped out. Recognition shone in her eyes as she hurried over to him.

"We got burgers and we went to the school. We watched movies together all night. You took me to the Cold Moon Ball, and I wore a purple dress. You were attacked trying to protect me." She slipped her arms around his waist. "And at the herbal shop, you kissed me. My first kiss. And you promised you'd come find me."

"And I did," Joe said, wanting desperately to kiss her in that moment. "I found you."

"Yes, you did. Now kiss me, Joseph Greg, or I might die."

He kissed her long and slow, thinking he never wanted to stop, thinking he never wanted to leave her, thinking he never wanted to be without her.

Thinking he could live like this forever.

EPILOGUE

*I*nfiniti peeled open her tired eyes and caught sight of the early summer sun filtering through her room. With a groan, she rolled her body away from the light and faced the wall. She'd only been in Havenwood Falls a few days, and each morning she had awoken exhausted with a racing pulse and a feeling of dread. She knew she'd been having crazy nightmarish dreams, but could never remember any of the details. Which was fine by her. She'd had enough chaos in her life to last her a good long while and didn't need any more. Even if it was in her sleep.

"Peace and happiness," she muttered to herself as she drew in a deep breath and stretched out her arms and legs. "And Joe."

She reached for the phone he had bought her and checked her messages. Sure enough, Joe had already texted.

Joe: Hey, beautiful. Text me when you're up

She smiled, her heart skipping a few beats as she thought of Joe. Eager to see him, she texted back.

Me: I'm up!

Joe: Can I come over? My mom made her special fritule pastries for you and Lyra

Infiniti had no idea what that was, but thought it sounded yummy. Plus, she'd be seeing Joe. She couldn't get enough of him.

Me: Yeah, come over
Joe: Ok, be there in a few

Flinging off her covers, she hurried to the bathroom. She splashed water on her face, ran her fingers through her long, wavy brown hair, then started brushing her teeth. She was in the middle of a gargle and spit when a knock sounded on the door.

"Hold on," she called out between the dribble, thinking there was no way that was Joe. He needed more time to get there, unless he had hauled ass, which was entirely possible.

She opened her bedroom door to find Lyra on the other side. Her host's short brown hair was tucked behind her ears and her usual pleasant smile was replaced with a worried expression.

"Infiniti, can you come to the living room? Addie is here and needs to speak to you."

"Addie?" Infiniti gulped.

Addie was Lyra's daughter. Infiniti didn't know Addie well, but the twenty-something woman had dropped by a few times since Infiniti had started staying there. She knew Addie worked for the mysterious Court of the Sun and the Moon. The only reason she was allowed to know this or anything about the Court was because of her own beyond-natural trips through time—and the fact that a wolf shifter was called to her.

"Uh, okay," Infiniti answered, suddenly nervous. "Let me change my clothes first."

"All right," Lyra said with a solemn nod.

Infiniti closed the door. She stood there for a while, wondering what the heck was going on, then quickly slipped out of her pajamas and into shorts and a T-shirt. A sinking feeling that she had done something wrong settled in her gut, even though she knew she hadn't done anything.

Dressed and ready for whatever Addie wanted, she entered the living room. Lyra and Addie were standing by the fireplace, talking in hushed voices. They fell silent when they spotted Infiniti.

"Um, good morning," Infiniti said with a half smile.

Addie's long brown hair was tied up in a loose bun. She eyed

Infiniti from over her dark-rimmed glasses. She was cool in a rocker chick kind of way with torn jeans and a healthy supply of tattoos, but also intimidating in a school principal kind of way. Infiniti wondered why she wanted to talk to her so early.

"Am I in trouble?" Infiniti asked with a nervous laugh. "Because with the way y'all are acting, it kind of feels like I am."

Before the mother-daughter duo could respond, the doorbell rang.

"Pretty sure that's Joe," Infiniti offered, relieved for him to be there because something was definitely up.

Addie eyed Lyra. "Guess he should hear this too."

"Yes," Lyra agreed. "It's good timing." She went to the door while Addie followed. Infiniti trailed behind, not wanting to miss anything.

"Um, good morning, Lyra," Joe said with a cocked brow when he saw the three of them at the door. He nodded toward Addie. "Good morning, Addie." He held up a tray wrapped in foil. "I've got some fritule from my mom. Enough for everyone."

Lyra took the tray. "Thank you, Joe. That's very kind of you and your mother. Why don't you come on inside? You're just in time for a special announcement from Addie."

Joe took Infiniti's hand and squeezed, tossing her a *what's going on* look. All she could do was shrug a little as they walked back to the living room and sat on the couch, because she was clueless.

Addie crossed her arms. She let a few seconds pass before she said, "We know it's you, Infiniti."

Tingles shot across Infiniti's skin while her mind scrambled for any clue to what Addie was talking about. "Huh?"

Lyra cut in. "But we also know you're not doing it on purpose."

Joe released Infiniti's hand and rose to his feet. "Hold on a second here. What are you talking about?"

Addie kept her focus on Infiniti. "Every night since Infiniti's arrival there have been space and time anomalies in the town."

Infiniti had been sitting, but stood up and joined Joe. Fear raced across her spine along with the realization that Addie was telling the truth. She had no idea what a space and time anomaly was, but she knew that whatever it was was connected to her because she'd been having crazy weird dreams since arriving and always woke up so drained.

Addie edged closer to Infiniti. "You know what I'm talking about, don't you?"

"Of course she doesn't," Joe asserted.

Infiniti took Joe's hand. She looked up at him. "I haven't been sleeping well since I got here, but I thought it was because of everything I'd been through." She turned her attention to Addie. "But I haven't been doing any space time whatever you said."

Addie's face softened. "You don't know that you have, but it's true. We've traced it to you."

Infiniti looked from Addie, to Lyra, to Joe, and then back to Addie. She was trying to process everything when Joe uttered, "Are you saying Infiniti has powers?"

Infiniti whipped her head in Joe's direction. Her mouth fell open. "Powers?"

"Yes," Addie answered. "That's exactly what we're saying."

"Probably from all of the time travel," Lyra added.

Addie nodded. "You need to learn about what you can do, as well as anything else that might have changed about you. Time travel is some freaky shit. And normally, we send young people who are awakening to their powers to night classes at the Sun and Moon Academy. But you're kind of old for that, and well, the timing just happens to work in your favor . . . anyway, the Court and I have come up with another idea." She narrowed her gaze on Infiniti and cocked her head. "If you can prove yourself."

Joe pulled Infiniti a little closer to him. An excited expression spread across his face.

"Addie, are you talking about SMA's College of Supernatural Guardians? Are you inviting Infiniti to test?"

"I sure am. The school has filled most of the spots for its inaugural class, but there's room for two more."

"*If* you can prove yourselves, that is," Lyra added.

Infiniti struggled to make sense of the information. "Wait a second. I'm not following."

Addie motioned to Joe so he could explain.

"It's a new college in town for supernaturals, but everyone who attends has to go through a series of trials. I was invited to test but turned it down because all I could do was focus on finding you. But now you're here, and you've got powers. So it appears we can both be tested now."

"Whoa," Infiniti whispered, hardly believing her ears. She had some sort of powers and could attend a college with Joe that had the words Supernatural Guardians in the name. She only had to pass a test or two first.

"Well, what do you say, Infiniti?" Addie asked. "It's either that or night classes at the Academy with the high schoolers. Your choice. But you have to decide quick, because the semester starts this month."

Excitement edged out Infiniti's nervousness as she thought of her favorite wizard movie where the students lived in a cool castle-like campus and had all kinds of magical adventures. She was totally down for something like that, especially if she could be with the guy she loved.

She smiled big at Joe, matching his emotions, and then faced Addie.

"I say sign me up."

We hope you enjoyed this story in the Havenwood Falls High series of novellas featuring a variety of supernatural creatures. The series is a collaborative effort by multiple authors.

Havenwood Falls books by Rose Garcia about Infiniti & Joe:

Saving Infiniti
Finding Infiniti

Sun & Moon Academy Book One: Fall Semester
Sun & Moon Academy Book Two: Spring Semester

Other books you might enjoy in the Young Adult Havenwood Falls High series:

Written in the Stars by Kallie Ross
Somewhere Within by Amy Hale
Bound by Shadows by Cameo Renae
Cast in Moonlight by Ali Winters

Stay up to date at www.HavenwoodFalls.com

ABOUT THE AUTHOR

Rose Garcia is the author of the critically acclaimed Final Life Series. The saga features gut-wrenching emotional turmoil and heart-stopping action with a diverse and dynamic cast. A lawyer turned writer, Rose has always been intrigued by science fiction and fantasy. More recently, she's been fascinated by a blend of science fiction and reality and the idea that some supernatural events are very real. Just ask her about the ghost she used to share a house with. Rose lives in Houston with her husband, two kids, and two dogs. Luckily, there are no ghosts in her current home. (That she knows of!) For information on Rose's releases and appearances, sign up for her newsletter at www.RoseGarciaBooks. com/newsletter. You can learn more about Rose at www. rosegarciabooks.com.

ACKNOWLEDGMENTS

WOW! My second installment in the Havenwood Falls High series has been born, and I have a ton of people to thank! First and foremost, I want to thank Kristie Cook, the amazing visionary, creator, and publisher of Havenwood Falls. I consider myself blessed that she invited me to bring my characters Infiniti and Fleet from the Final Life Series to her supernatural town. It's been a wild ride, and I look forward to cranking out many more stories with her phenomenal team!

To all the Havenwood Falls authors who helped me breathe life into my story: Kallie Ross who shared many of her characters with me including Joseph Greg and his family, Sheriff Ric and Kase of the Kasun pack, and Rose Howe; Justine Winter who let me set the deadly duo of reaper Shade StormIron and Death on Infiniti's heels; SF Benson who helped me SO much with my Death scenes; E.J. Fechenda who created Dr. Underwood; and Kristie Cook who created Lyra Beaumont. I have a super cool Court of the Sun and the Moon scene which includes Kristie Cook's Addie Beaumont and Saundra Beaumont; Morgan Wylie's Lilith Blackstone and Mathilde Augustine; Amy Hale's Lawrence Mills; Randi Cooley Wilson's Roman Bishop; E.J. Fechenda's Elsmed Fairchild, and T.V. Hahn's Barbie Stuart and Teeny Weeny Tahini. I loved writing this scene so much!

A huge thanks to Regina Wamba for my gorgeous cover and Liz Ferry for her eagle eye editing! And, of course, to my awesome publicist Amber Garcia.

And last, but not least, to my amazing beta readers and

critique partners who've been a part of my writing journey for many years: Heather Elliot, Jessica Ramirez, Olivia Moriarty, and Wade Moriarty. You guys ROCK!

But all the thanks really go to my amazing readers. Especially those in my FB reader group, Rose's Rebels. Thank you for your support, friendship, and encouragement! I hope you enjoyed *Finding Infiniti*!

AN EXCERPT

Unicorn's Lament (A Havenwood Falls High Novella) by Megan Linski

From *USA Today* Bestselling Author Megan Linski - she might be a girly girl, but she never imagined being an actual unicorn princess—or that her own mother would seek to destroy her.

Thea has no idea what her future holds. When she's whisked off to a mysterious town in the mountains, she finds out magic is real—and so are unicorns.

If that wasn't shocking enough, she also learns that her mom's an evil sorceress who desires to destroy the unicorns, and all of Havenwood Falls is in danger. Thea has until her eighteenth birthday to learn how to control her magic, lead the herd, and maybe kiss the cute girl at Havenwood Stables.

UNICORN'S LAMENT

BY MEGAN LINSKI

The same dream haunted me every night.

I followed the silver unicorn through the gray, misty forest. I never got quite close enough to see many details, but I knew he was a stallion—he had huge muscles and stood at a height that would tower over me, if I dared to get near. His coat was shinier than the edge of a sharpened knife, and his rippling mane and tail went past his knees.

But the most incredible thing about him was the golden horn that stuck out of the middle of his forehead. It shimmered and sparkled, even in the cloudy day, and seemed to gleam when he looked toward me.

I chased the stallion through the woods. But though I ran as fast as I could, winding through trees and ducking branches, the unicorn was always faster. Just as I was about to reach out and pet his coat, he raced off into the trees and vanished.

Then I woke up.

I started upright in bed. My chest heaved as if I'd been running. I took a few deep breaths and tried to steady myself.

Just another dream, Thea. It's not real.

I hated that it wasn't real. Something about that unicorn made me feel empty inside without him.

But unicorns weren't real, and neither were dreams. Shaking off how vivid it felt, I stumbled out of bed and forced myself to take a cold shower, allowing the water to roll down my back, trying to wake myself up.

I couldn't. Even though I tried, the dream followed me around all day.

Havenwood Village was a nice apartment complex—certainly the best I'd ever lived in. I liked that I had my own bathroom. My mom had landed a good job at the Havenwood Falls Medical Center, and for the first time in a long while, we were doing fine.

First time since the fire, I guess.

I threw my white-blond hair up into a ponytail, slipping on a pair of jeans and a racerback top. I longed to grab the pink dress and sparkly heels in the corner of my closet and change into that instead, but I reminded myself that wasn't who I was anymore.

Ambrosia was already at the stove in the kitchen, making pancakes.

"How did you sleep, honey?" she asked as I sat at the table, placing a stack of pancakes in front of me. They were topped with raspberries, whipped cream, and sprinkles, just how I liked them.

"Fine, Ambrosia," I lied. My mother never wanted me to call her Mom, just always by her first name. It'd been like that since I was a little girl. It was a little weird to some people, but I was used to it.

She noticed the bags under my eyes and said, "You should be sleeping in. School will start pretty soon, and you won't be able to."

"I know." It was early August. My eighteenth birthday was thirty days away, at the end of the month. I'd be starting my senior year at Havenwood Falls High soon.

I hated starting a new school this close to graduation, but at the same time, Havenwood Falls High couldn't possibly be worse than Desmona Prep back in the Big Easy. That place had been hell on earth.

"Why don't you go to the lake later? There are plenty of people your age swimming, I'd bet. It's going to be such a nice day," Ambrosia suggested.

"I'm not one much for friends." I liked to keep to myself. I shoveled my pancakes into my mouth and enjoyed every bite of them. Yep. Solitude and food. Peace, quiet, and sweets were all a girl needed.

"You know," Ambrosia started, and she sat down on the other side of the table to eat her own pancakes, "I heard there's a riding stable nearby."

That piqued my interest. "Really?"

"Yep. Trains jumpers." She reached around to the drawers behind her, pulled open one of them, and handed me a brochure. I read it quickly.

Havenwood Stables. Looked like a fancy place, the kind where Olympians would train. I hadn't ridden a horse since I'd left Desmona Prep. I was dying to get back on one again. "How much do they charge?"

"What if I told you I already paid for a full semester's worth of lessons?" Ambrosia held her mug of coffee and smiled.

"No freaking way!" I shouted. "Ambrosia, you're the best!"

I got up and hugged her. It only took a few minutes for me to rush back into my room, change into a pair of breeches and knee-high boots, and grab my riding helmet.

"It's close enough you can walk," Ambrosia said. She got out a map of the town, took a red marker, and drew a path before she handed it to me.

I grabbed it and headed for the door. I was practically running to get there.

"Stick to the main road," Ambrosia warned me. She sounded serious about it. "Don't go into the woods. I mean it."

"Yes, Ambrosia." I hurried outside. It was still early morning, and a bit chilly out. I should've grabbed a jacket. I shivered, hoping the temperature would get back up to the forecasted seventy-five quick. The climate was way different here than it was in Louisiana. I was used to frying out there. Here I'd have to deal with snow, something I'd hardly seen before. I was a bit nauseated from the high altitude, though it was beginning to subside now that I was up and moving.

As I walked, I took in the sights of my new home. It was small, but Havenwood Falls was a nice place. Idyllic. Charming, even. But it was more than a little weird. The vibe that came off of it was . . . odd. It was nothing like New Orleans, which I missed, but not enough to want to go back.

I thought it wasn't a quiet town, either. I'd only been living here a few days, but just from walking around the area, I got the sense that every resident here had some kind of secret to hide.

I looked at the map Ambrosia had drawn. The stables were to the west, just outside of town. I could stick to the main road, as she said, and get there most likely in a half hour or so.

But it looked like there was a shortcut I could take—near the woods by the Mathews River. It seemed like rough terrain, but I bet it'd cut my walk time in half.

I was never very good at following the rules, so I left the sidewalk and veered into the trees, crossing over a creek by way of a small homemade bridge someone had built. I had a good sense of direction and could tell which way was west, so I kept walking that way, figuring I'd hit the horse stables sooner or later.

It didn't take me long to realize that I was lost. But I didn't mind it. I liked wandering. There's something nice about feeling like you are the only person in the world. I enjoyed my walk through the greenery, taking in the smells of fresh morning dew on the pine trees and listening to the birds chirping.

Then I heard something—the crack of a branch.

I whirled around. My eyes went wide when I saw what was standing above me.

On an embankment overhead stood a horse—but it wasn't a horse at all. It was the unicorn. Even more, it was *my* unicorn, and he was real. He stood proudly, his head held high and his ears pointing toward me. His silver coat shone in a halo of light the sun had formed around him, and his golden horn glistened, just like it did in my dream. His nostrils flared as he observed me, taking me in.

I took a step forward. But as soon as I moved, the unicorn took off and disappeared into the trees.

I stood there frozen for a few seconds, struggling to comprehend what had just happened. Yeah. Havenwood Falls was definitely different.

Purchase *Unicorn's Lament* where books are sold.